PONIES ON THE TRAIL

This Armada book belongs to:

_____

_____

_____

Diana Pullein-Thompson grew up in Oxfordshire in a family of four children. They all learned to ride when they were very small, and their first mount was Countess, a retired polo pony, whom they used to climb on to by stepladder. Diana left school at fourteen, and, with her two sisters, started the Grove Riding School, which inspired some of her early books and eventually grew into a large establishment with forty-two horses and ponies. She has written over twenty books, and her sisters, Christine and Josephine, are also well-known as children's writers. She is married to art historian and museum director, Dennis Farr, and they live in Warwickshire with their two children, two dogs, two tortoises, a hamster, guinea pig and tame rat. They also have a grey pony called Jupiter.

PONIES ON THE TRAIL

DIANA PULLEIN-THOMPSON

An Armada Original

Ponies On the Trail was first published in Armada
in 1978 by Fontana Paperback,
14 St. James's Place, London SW1A 1PS

This impression 1979

© Diana Pullein-Thompson 1978

Printed in Great Britain by
Love & Malcomson Ltd., Brighton Road,
Redhill, Surrey.

CONTENTS

1. THE BEGINNING   9
2. MONDAY   18
3. TUESDAY   33
4. WEDNESDAY   45
5. THURSDAY   60
6. FRIDAY   77
7. SATURDAY   94

CHAPTER ONE

THE BEGINNING

"An adventure holiday, that's what they call it nowadays," said Jake, giving us a quizzical smile. "With Offa's Dyke into the bargain. I shall be glad of your help."

"Of course," we said, sitting on the rickety iron gate of Jake's stable yard and swinging our legs. "Silverstar and Mimosa will love it."

Jake was one of our favourite grown-ups. He had come to the rescue when we had moved from the town to the country and bought a pony without knowing much about stable management. At the end of last summer we had started helping him with his pony trekking business, and during the winter we had sometimes ridden up to his place to talk about this and that.

"Not under canvas, can't stand tents," Jake went on, leaning against the door of a shed, "but in barns up in the hills, the old shepherds' huts, in sleeping bags. I'm having the saddles fitted with extra dees. Just a dozen or so riders, and we provide the lot—pony, food, and equipment for six days."

"Great, brilliant!" said Fergie. "Do we get free grub?"

"Free everything for you and Sandy, so long as you work, help with the cooking and the saddling-up and so on."

"And stop the ponies grazing with the beginners," I added, having experienced that difficulty on all-day pony treks.

"Middle of May, you said, didn't you?" asked my brother. "That fits in with our half term. We'll write it down in the diary as soon as we get home. I suppose that snow will have shifted by then." He glanced towards a great shoulder of hill whose top shone white in the watery blue light that comes over the Shropshire hills after rain. In the distance were the snow-capped mountains of Wales. Up here on Offa's Dyke there is a magic in the air that I have met nowhere else, but, like most elements of the spirit, is felt only by those who are open to it.

"I hope some girls come," said Fergie after a pause. "I mean, don't adventure holidays appeal mostly to middle-aged people wanting to recapture their youth, and to teen-age boys wanting to prove themselves?"

"Can't say. Never tried. Have to wait and see, won't we?" Jake grinned again. "Might get an odd bunch, bearded weirdies, long-haired layabouts, or a really nice lot. That's part of the adventure for us. I need you specially because there's them that don't understand our speech. And there's them from Glasgow or London or other such places that I can't make 'ead or tail of."

"Sort of interpreters?" I suggested.

"That's it, and there are sure to be one or two daft ones in the party, there always are."

"But not all long-haired boys are layabouts, and Dad's growing a beard and he's no weirdie," put in Fergie, who at fourteen and a half felt old enough to question one or two of Jake's assertions.

"Well, I'm not saying you couldn't be right there." Jake straightened up from his relaxed position against the door. "Want to see the mare I bought from Jim Stubbard? A bit wild now, but she'll quieten down with work."

"Love to," we said.

We got down from the gate and went into Jake's stone

and timber barn. And there was the mare standing in the corner, munching hay, her bay hindquarters round as an apple, her broad tail black as ebony.

"Maybe she's too good for trekking. I don't know, can't tell yet," said Jake. "She's quiet enough to handle, but she doesn't half take hold when she feels grass under her feet. Stubbard's grandson has been galloping like a crazy cowboy, I shouldn't wonder. He had the idea he might hunt, so they stabled and corn-fed her all winter and then that young man changed his mind and bought one of those Suzuki bikes instead. Here, come on, let's see you."

Jake's marvellously soft voice with its Welsh lilt made the mare turn towards him at once. She gazed at us with great eyes shining like black treacle in the grey light of the barn. Her wide forehead, decorated with a star, tapered to a delicate muzzle with a snip of white between the nostrils. Bright and polished as a cherished conker, she boasted black points and four neat black hoofs. Solidly built, with short cannon bones, long thighs and forearms and a deep girth, she still had about her an unmistakeable air of breeding.

"Part thoroughbred?" I suggested.

"Maybe, but she's got no papers. Gentle as a kitten she is. Lovely shoulder she's got, hasn't she? I've called her Treasure. Thought I'd drop the chocolates and sweets and go on to precious stones and metals . . . Copper, Garnet, Pearl, Ruby, Peridot, that sort of thing." Jake gave the mare a handful of oats from a bulging pocket, and added, "I'm going to ride her on the trail myself."

A door opened in the grey farmhouse and Jake's rather gaunt wife looked out.

"Your tea's ready," she called. "It'll be getting cold if you don't come in directly."

The chipped brown door shut again with a sharpness

11

which suggested impatience. Jake's wife has never shared his interest in horses, and Fergie and I could never quite see why she had married him, but our parents said she had the features of a past beauty and the remnants of an entrancing voice, and an enraptured Jake was not the sort of man to take no for an answer.

"We must be off," I said hastily. "And thanks. Of course, count on us to help with the adventure trip."

We turned towards our ponies who had been standing tied to a fence. Mimosa, who is a palomino mare, looked round and gave a sweet little whinny of welcome, and Silverstar pawed the ground with a neat grey foreleg as though trying to tell us her patience was coming to an end.

"One of Jake's brainwaves!" said Fergie, mounting Silverstar.

"Twelve people. Not bad. He could make a few hundred, pounds, but the food will cost a lot, I expect," I replied, turning Mimosa towards home.

Dusk was falling, hiding the hills one by one, as we rode down the lane.

"I suppose Mum and Dad will agree," I wondered, in sudden doubt.

"They trust Jake absolutely, you know that," said Fergie. "Let's trot."

At home, Mimosa's foal, now a yearling, let out a long neigh of welcome as we turned into the yard. Leary, our tri-coloured collie, bounded forward to meet us, and Mummy called from a window, "There's warm lardy cake for tea if you hurry."

I felt suddenly that life was good and the future full of splendid opportunities.

Within ten days Jake's advertisement had appeared in one national and two local papers.

PONIES ON THE TRAIL (it began)
Adventure holiday in the Welsh Marches.
Ride all day and sleep out under the stars, warmed
by camp fires. 6 days. All details on application.

"Old Jake's got a touch of the romantic in him," said
Dad, looking at the advertisement over my shoulder. "It's
quite an original approach to what is, after all, just a
longer version of his usual trek."

"He's a poet at heart, that's why he loves this place,"
said Mum. "Listen, if you are going to help him you must
be responsible. Do you remember the first aid I taught
you? You mustn't muck about or quarrel with each other.
You may be dealing with adults." She looked at us sternly
with blue eyes, a frown between her brows.

"You're talking to us as though we were two of your
infants at school," I objected. "I'm nearly thirteen and
Fergie's not far off fifteen and once upon a time girls of
my age became nursery maids and were trusted with the
babies of rich ladies."

"Sandy's right," Dad said, "and they've got two
damned good ponies. People don't become responsible
until they're given responsibility."

"Point taken," said Mummy. "Now, Fergie, would you
pick the last of the sprouts? And, Sandy, be an angel
and see whether my wee hens have obliged with any eggs?"

We let a week pass before we rode up to the top of the
Dyke to see Jake. Had he received one or a hundred
replies? We felt his sort of advertisement led to extremes.

"A stack," he told us. "Seems there are a fair number
of people wanting to sleep under the stars. Why they
can't do it in their back garden beats me. I've answered
the first ten and left the others till I see how things go.

13

It's a risky business when you don't know the sort of people you're going to get. But I've asked them to give me the fullest details of themselves."

"Part of the adventure," we chanted.

"What do they *sound* like?" asked Fergie.

"Well, there are several girls," said Jake, winking at me.

"Sounds promising," said Fergie, looking unmoved. "Though I'm not particularly interested in girls at the moment."

"And there's a man—sounds Russian or Bulgarian, or Polish, I shouldn't wonder. Igor something or another."

"A spy?" I hazarded.

"Go on, who else?" urged Fergie. "Don't keep us in suspense."

"Couple of girls who work in the same office in a place called Croydon, near London it seems. They've done a bit of trekking in Sussex."

"Any children?"

"Couple of kids, but I've put them aside. Don't want anyone under fourteen, bar Sandy. There's a professor and his wife, and a kind of student, and I can't remember who the others are. Oh, wait a minute, there's a Swedish girl of sixteen. She sent a photo, wanted to be sure she was saved a place on the trail. Here, hang on."

Jake rustled in his pocket and brought out a coloured snapshot with a few damp oats stuck to it. "There, what do you think of her, eh?"

The photograph showed a blonde girl with a slightly tip-tilted nose sitting on a beach in a bikini. Her skin was golden as honey and her eyes grape hyacinth blue. It was the sort of picture you might expect to find on the cover of a magazine.

"Crumbs!" cried Fergie. "She looks like Miss World. She doesn't look like a camping sort of person."

"Have to wait and see, won't we?" said Jake. "There's no telling is there?" He dug deeper in his pocket, saying, "I've made a list of some of the ponies we shall take," and brought out a crumpled piece of paper on which he had written in a beautiful, old-fashioned looped hand. *Toffee, Caramelo, Bournville, Fudge, Peppermint, Twix, Cadbury, Rolo, Crunchie, Sandyfloss, Treasure, Bullfinch, Sandpiper.*

The last two he had owned in the days when he had named all his ponies after birds, before the chocolate and sweet era. He rarely kept any pony for more than a few years because he was always willing to sell one if the right kind of owner came along offering a fair price.

"I reckon Toffee and Fudge will be just right for the office girls who don't seem to know much, seeing it takes a bit of effort to get them into a canter."

"As long as they don't keep grazing," I muttered.

"The professor gives the weight and height of both himself and his wife—there's a bit of sense for a change—mite of a man he must be at nine stone six, but he says he's tough and accustomed to hill walking. I thought of Sandpiper for him. His wife rode as a girl, he tells me, but she's a biggish woman, over ten stone, he says. Funny how little men go for large women. Who shall we give her?"

"Bournville," I suggested, for having had the loan of the liver chestnut for a winter, I knew that he was both steady and kind.

"And the Swedish girl? She claims to have ridden only in the ménage, but can jump four feet and has competed in dressage. Sounds quite a plucky girl."

"Maybe a swank," said Fergie. "What about Caramelo, she's got a bit of zip about her."

"Right . . . Caramelo, and we'll put her in *your* charge,"

15

said Jake, writing on a corner of the paper with a chipped black biro.

Jake's enthusiasm was catching. We tied up Silverstar and Mimosa, and leaned against a shed and planned. Spring was in the air, and little clouds scudded across a breezy sky like the sails of ships against a grey sea.

Most of Jake's ponies were out on loan for another week, then, with the Easter holidays starting, and the pony trekking season about to begin, he wanted us to come over and help see that they were fit and in good trim. We would ride them each in turn and, if any seemed particularly fresh, take them for a two or three hour hack. In return, Jake would transport our ponies to local shows for us in his cattle truck, and tack on any cast shoes when we couldn't get quickly to the blacksmith in Ludlow. He had started training as a blacksmith at fourteen before going into lorry driving, so he knew how to rasp and where to hammer in the nails. His own ponies seemed to survive a summer of his shoeing, but were mostly ridden on grass so the strain wasn't great, and then, in the winter, those who borrowed them saw that they were professionally shod.

After we had talked for a while I schooled Silverstar. because I had entered her for a pony club dressage test in the holidays. She is a lovely pony, beautifully dappled and pretty as porcelain, with a long neck and sloping shoulders, so that she seems much bigger than fourteen-two which is her actual height. Fergie put up bean poles and practised bending on Mimosa because he had hopes of being chosen to represent our branch of the pony club in the Prince Philip Cup. Mimosa is rather wide and strong-willed, but once she has found she can't get her own way, she tries her best. She has a lovely head, with very big soft eyes, and lots of lovely flaxen hair which we leave long so that she has a tail almost sweeping the ground and a forelock reaching to her eyelashes. Our pony club instructress, called Henrietta Turnstile, is always telling us to pull them, but Fergie loves Mimosa to look like a wild pony from the moors resembling a drawing by Seaby, and always refuses. I don't know whether we are right, but at least Mimosa does seem better able to cope with the flies than Silverstar, whose mane and tail are a conventional length.

It was Saturday morning, a lovely day with the green grass sprouting in the meadows and shining in the brown bracken on the hillsides. A watery spring sun touched everything with the palest gold, so that even the cobwebs on the thorn hedges glistened. And the village was noisy with lambs bleating, ewes calling, a forlorn cow mooing for a lost calf, and the deep throated crowing of Mummy's new big red cockerel as he stood high on a three-quarter gate and proclaimed his kingship of our fields and his ten plump wives.

CHAPTER TWO

MONDAY

"That's it," said Jake. "Fifteen sleeping bags, thirty saddle bags. Quite a capital outlay, but if I can run two adventure holidays each year between lambing and harvest, I'll be doing nicely. Now you check the sandwiches. There should be two full rounds in fifteen bags; the other bags are for clothes. Oh, and a chocolate Penguin, too."

"Drinks?" asked Fergie.

"From the streams and springs, natural like. This is an adventure, not a ride to a luxury hotel."

"But there will be meals every evening? I mean where's *that* food coming from?" I said.

Jake put a finger to his head and pretended to turn a screwdriver. "I'm all right," he said. "I'm not round the bend yet. If I starve them they won't survive. At each stop there will be food, beer and a spot of cider for the ladies."

"What about the sex discrimination act?"

"They can have beer if they like. I'm not particular."

"We'll drink what no one else wants," said Fergie. "The leftovers."

"You'll not drink at all, you're under age," retorted Jake with a grin. "Now let's get the ponies saddled. They'll all be here soon, likely as not, and we want to look efficient, don't we?"

Jake had split the ride into three groups, so that we each had four ponies and riders to look after. Fearing that the

18

older people might not care to be guided by teenagers, as we called ourselves for want of a better word, he had put Professor and Mrs. Gray, a widow named Helen Wetherall and a librarian, called Eric Small, who sounded fussy, in his group.

I was to be in charge of the two typists, the Russian, who, Jake said, would be courteous to a girl, and the student, Jonathan Smith, who wrote long letters in a spiky hand.

Fergie was to look after the Swedish girl, Kristianne, a sixteen-year-old, Michael Appleby, who was hoping to go to sixth form college, and twin sisters, Felicity and Jane Woodfield. Jake said the young women would be likely to take notice of an attractive male, which made Fergie turn the colour of a morello cherry, as he is not nearly as sophisticated as he likes to think.

Fergie and I had decided to swop ponies at lunchtime every day, with me starting with Silverstar.

Eight of the riders, whom Dad fetched in his mini-bus from Ludlow Station, were soon with us. Then Professor and Mrs. Gray arrived in an old Morris Cambridge, and Michael Appleby chugged up the lane on a brand new moped. "My reward for getting nine O. Levels," he explained when we admired it.

Jake ticked names off on a list written on the back of an old brown envelope. "Still one missing—the student— one of yours, Sandy," he said, as though I were responsible.

"How was he coming?" asked Professor Gray in a slightly squeaky voice.

"Got his letter back at the house. I'll go and look. Fergie, see the ponies are all right, will you?" Jake tried to look unperturbed.

"Students are normally half an hour late these days,"

said Mrs. Gray, sticking another hairpin into her bun. "It's their way of life."

"That's not quite fair, dear," said her husband, "there *are* exceptions."

"Hitching," said Jake, coming out of the house. "Like as not he's still in Kidderminster, or waiting on the other side of Shrewsbury."

"I think hitch-hiking is immoral," said the widow, Helen Wetherall. "It's begging, isn't it?"

No one answered, and soon Fergie and I started introducing the riders to their mounts. We could tell whether or not they knew much about animals by the way they approached their ponies.

Half an hour later Jonathan Smith came wandering up the lane with a dreamy look on his face as though time was not important. He was a weedy young man in his mid-twenties, with a thin, straw-coloured beard cut to a point, watery blue eyes, and thinning long fair hair.

"Mr. Smith?" enquired Jake, who does not mince words. "We're all waiting for you."

"Is it really past twelve o'clock? My watch has stopped. I couldn't get a hitch after Ludlow," he mumbled, avoiding Jake's stern gaze.

"Can we mount now?" asked Professor Gray, pushing his bi-focal glasses more firmly on his nose.

"Yes, all up, if you please," said Jake.

Jonathan Smith took some time to sort out his clothes, and then I held Rolo, who is fifteen hands and lively, for him to mount. He climbed on slowly and held the reins hopelessly, like a beginner, so that they hung in loops.

"Ridden before?"

"Not for years."

"Well, squeeze with your calves to make him move on

20

or go faster, and straighten your back and tighten your hold on the reins when you want him to stop. If that doesn't do the trick you may have to pull. All right?"

"Sort of," he mumbled, looking uncomfortable.

"Rolo's quite lively," I warned. "But Jake decided from your letter that you could gallop and even jump a bit."

"Perhaps I misled him a little. I was feeling optimistic at the time, always a dangerous mood," muttered Jonathan.

"Well, anyway, let me show you how to hold the reins. Look, like this."

When all the members of my group were mounted and ready to start I looked at them with some alarm. Could I ever control them? Wasn't I too young? The Russian, Igor Polunsky, was dark and bearded with very bright, almost black, eyes. He waved his arms when he spoke and sprang into the saddle with such energy that he nearly went over the other side.

The typists, Valerie and Linda, had the pallor of London girls who watched their weight, ate too little and worked in over-heated offices. Otherwise they were quite different from one another. Valerie was mouse-haired with a turned-up nose and slightly sticking-out teeth, and Linda was rather pretty, with regular features, dark brown hair tied in a ponytail, and violet-blue eyes hedged with long lashes. They both had very long fingernails painted green, wore much grey-green eyeshadow, and arrived carrying dainty handbags, which Jake told them must be left with his wife at the farmhouse.

"Can't have vanity sets out riding," he said with a grin. "Everything's got to be carried in the saddle bags or rolled up in front of the saddle. This is an adventure ride, not a beauty competition." They had not been offended, because they had at once branded him as a *character*.

They were mounted thus:

21

Valerie—Toffee; Linda—Fudge; Igor Polunsky—Cadbury; Jonathan—Rolo.

The first two ponies were both liver chestnut mares by the same Welsh sire. Fudge had two white socks and a wide white blaze which made her face seem wider than it was. Toffee was slightly darker and absolutely plain, bar a tiny snippet of white between her nostrils. Cadbury was a dark bay, with black points and a sensible, slightly heavy, head with a white star and trickle, and Rolo a rather narrow dun with a lean head, large hollows above his eyes and a black list down his back. Jake always favoured bays, liver chestnuts, duns and roans, believing that these colours denoted hardiness.

At half-past twelve we set off, an hour late, up the muddy track that led to the top of the hill, Jake leading the way on Treasure who was bouncy and inclined to shy. Fergie's group came second, and I brought up the rear.

"He puts you last because you're a girl," Jonathan said. "Nomadic man always made the woman follow, and there's something of the gipsy about Jake, isn't there?"

"I don't know," I said. "His people have belonged to the village for years. He runs a trekking centre, farms a bit, and transports cattle."

The Professor looked very merry riding up at the front with Jake, gesticulating as he talked. He was a little man, wiry with a funny short nose with a blob at the end and rather bulging eyes. Treasure's ears were back and she kept snatching at the bit and swishing her tail. She wanted to lead and resented the good-natured Sandpiper, plodding beside her with his big hooves making a lovely squelchy noise in the mud.

Fergie's group seemed very orderly at first. Kristianne was managing the lovely palomino, Caramelo, with great aplomb, riding like a well-taught continental with definite contact on her pony's mouth, a very straight back and bent calf, her chin up and her beautiful blonde hair curled into a loose bun. She looked to me as though she had been brought up on eggs, honey, cream and nectar, and I suspect every girl in the party wished they could have been given her appearance. I was also terribly envious of her riding. Why had she come?

"I love riding," she was saying, "and the exercise is good for me. I love adventure—it is good. And I love the English," she flashed a smile at Fergie and Michael Appleby. "It was as simple as that," she added, pleased that she knew so colloquial a phrase.

"Sweden has one of the highest suicide rates in the world," Jonathan told me gloomily. "So don't be misled by looks."

Up and up we went until I thought we must become part of the sky itself. Then, reaching the ridge, we paused to look down on a patchwork world below.

"There's our house," said Fergie, turning Mimosa. "It looks like part of a toy farmyard."

"Where? Please show me—I want to know," said Kristianne.

Fudge started to graze, throwing down her head so suddenly that Linda took a dive and landed in the wet green grass with a little shriek.

"Adventure number one," said Professor Gray.

"Do not laugh, she might be hurt," retorted Igor Polunsky.

"No bones broken!" To my relief Linda got up laughing. "Why did he do that?"

"She suddenly felt hungry. Be ready next time."

I jumped off and helped Linda remount. "I used to do exactly the same when I started," I told her. "Mimosa was a devil for grass."

We rode on with the sun shining on our backs and all the scents of May around us, high on the green ridge looking across to Wales.

"I feel near heaven. Put out your hand and you might touch God," said the Russian, smiling through the dark thicket of his beard.

"Let's gallop," cried Professor Gray. "Have a race, lay bets."

"But I would win. I am the fittest, I have the best horse and perhaps the most experience," said Kristianne coolly. "I ride in a ménage four hours a week, and I swim three and work in a gymnasium as well."

"Oh dear, she's one of those keep-fit girls. I can't bear them," mumbled Jonathan. "My legs are tired. And Rolo keeps pulling."

"That's because you're holding him too tight. He needs more rein," I said.

"He'll gallop off."

"No he won't."

The Professor was not to be forgotten.

"How about it, Mr. . . . ?"

"Everyone calls me Jake. No, not yet, Professor. A little patience. Not everyone here will stay stuck on at a gallop. You and the beauty queen and a few others can hang back with Fergie a little further on and then have a go. But I shouldn't race. It hots the ponies up something terrible."

"*Your* ride, of course, as *you* say," said the Professor. "You know your animals."

"May I stretch my legs?" asked Eric Small, the librarian. "They feel a little taxed to say the least."

"Of course."

After several riders had walked around for a while, we continued quietly down until lunchtime, when we stopped in a dell surrounded by mountain ash and one or two gorse bushes, through which a stream trickled merrily over brown boulders. We took plastic cups out of our saddle bags, dipped them in the water and drank deep.

"I only hope there is not a dead sheep further up. I should hate to die of typhoid," remarked Eric Small. He was a tallish man, pale-faced, with stone grey eyes and receding hair cut short against his head. "This won't please my dental surgeon," he added, as he bit into his penguin. "Chocolate, tut, tut."

"There's iron in chocolate, that's why mountaineers take it with them on long climbs," said Jonathan.

We changed the ponies bridles for head-collars and they dragged their riders hither and thither in search of the juiciest clumps of grass. A little mist gathered like cob-webs on the hilltops. It was two o'clock.

By three we were mounted and on our way, with Eric exclaiming that his 'posterior' was a little sore. Mrs. Grey made sympathetic noises and Jake said, "I've got some methylated spirits for sore backsides."

"That sounds dreadfully primitive," said the librarian.

"Well, salt's just as good, if you prefer that."

"Now what about that promised gallop?" asked the Professor. "We've not gone out of a trot so far."

"True enough," said Jake, "but I wanted to give you and your ponies time to settle down with one another." (Some of Jake's animals were, of course, horses, but with trekking, as with polo, there are some people who refer to them all as ponies, whatever their size.)

"You see that track there," Jake pointed, then paused while he lit a cigarette. "When we reach it, you and Fergie and anyone else who wants a bit of speed-racing stay back until we are way ahead and then follow like the wind."

"Like the wind!" said the Professor delightedly. "As

fast as the wind! Who else?" he turned, lithe as a monkey, in the saddle, "Who else is for a gallop? Speak up, or for ever hold your peace."

"I think my posterior has had quite sufficient for today, thank you," said Eric Small.

"Me, me," cried Felicity and Jane, in unison.

"I will join you, of course," said Kristianne.

"Maybe I shall fall, but I will," added Igor Polunsky, as though it were a matter of honour.

"Is Bournville quiet? I mean he doesn't buck or anything?"

"No, Mrs. Gray. It would be hard to find a steadier horse anywhere."

"Well, then, I shall ride on with Geoffrey."

So we left those seven behind and continued on our way.

"I'll go next time," said Michael Appleby. "I'm a bit loose in the saddle. I say, doesn't that Swedish girl ride beautifully."

We must have covered an eighth of a mile before we heard the thunder of hooves behind us. Looking round, I saw Caramelo in the lead, with the Professor second, using his stick on Cadbury and waving his elbows up and down. Hot in pursuit raced Felicity and Jane neck and neck on Crunchie and Peppermint, two dumpling ponies who wore cruppers to stop their saddles going over their heads. Behind them came Bournville, steady and kind, with Mrs. Gray looking exhausted and insecure.

"Rather her than me," said Helen Wetherall, smiling her rather plaintive smile which revealed the top row of an excellent set of false teeth. "She's a brave lady."

Kristianne brought Caramelo to an elegant halt a few yards from us, and with a yelp of glee the Professor raced on and past us.

"A madcap," said Jake.

The twins' ponies, seeing that the end was near, broke thankfully into a trot. Mrs. Gray hauled rather frantically at Bournville who stopped at once, and Cadbury followed suit. The Russian mopped his brow, muttering, "Super, super." Sandpiper swung back, and the Professor landed in deep grass.

"Geoffrey, Geoffrey, you are too wild," lamented his wife. "I saw it coming."

But the man leapt to his feet like a jack-in-the-box, and then went down on all fours and started to search frantically through the grass.

"His glasses," said Mrs. Gray. "He can hardly see without them."

Fergie, who had arrived after the others at a collected canter, dismounted to help while I caught Sandpiper.

"Adventure number two," said Igor Polunsky, running a hand through his beard.

"He asked for it, whooping like that," said Jake disapprovingly. Fergie found the spectacles and mercifully they were unbroken, and then we continued down towards the farm building where we were to spend the first night. The men were to sleep in a loft and the women in a couple of stables below. Both had been cleaned out and bedded down in deep straw.

"Will there be rats?" asked Linda.

"Straw usually harbours livestock, lice and fleas. I hope you have your supply of D.D.T." said Eric Small.

"You didn't expect luxury hotels, did you?" asked Jake. "And you are welcome to sleep outside, if you prefer that."

"Of course not, but the gap between a luxury hotel and this is about a hundred miles."

"I think it's most exciting," declared Helen Wetherall

unexpectedly. "We can pretend we are Highlanders after the '45, hiding from the Redcoats, and wrap ourselves in our plaids, bury ourselves deep in the straw—only it would have been dried bracken—and dream the dreams of heroes."

Sacks of oats and bran were awaiting us and a stack of buckets. After drinking deep at a trough and being unsaddled and bridled, the ponies gobbled their feeds before being turned out in a big meadow.

. "Now, what about nosh for us? I'm starving," said Michael Appleby, who was a pugnacious-looking boy with shortish dark hair and plump lips.

"Now the cooks go into action," said Jake, looking at us.

Two fireplaces had been roughly constructed out of bricks in a sheltered corner away from the prevailing wind, and, in the stable, bags of sausages and chips, bread, tomatoes and a can of oil awaited us, all stacked in large two-handled metal jam-making saucepans. Jake lit the fires, assisted by Michael, and Fergie and I cooked, helped by the twins, Felicity and Jane, who chattered happily about the drawbacks of their comprehensive school and the unrivalled excellence of the riding establishment where they rode. They were very friendly, with cheerful, slightly freckled faces framed by rather untidy, fuzzy fair hair which hung in forelocks above lively blue eyes. They said Peppermint and Crunchie were terrific, and they were not frightened of fleas and mice, and if a rat came they would try to tame him, as prisoners had in dungeons years ago.

"Bravo!" cried Mrs. Wetherall. "You are people after my own heart."

Soon Jake was busy handing out beer and cider; tired riders were sitting round the fires and smiling, and the soft light of dusk lay on the hills. The sausages and chips cooked beautifully, and seemed to taste deliciously of woodsmoke when we ate them. For pudding there were little plastic cartons of trifle from some supermarket refrigerator, which didn't seem quite right in the circumstances.

"Where did it all come from?" asked Mrs. Gray.

"The fairies," said Jake with a smile. "The good fairies who looked after the great King Offa's army."

A couple of oil hurricane lanterns had also arrived with the supplies, and soon these were lit. The Russian wanted to sing, but Jonathan said a sing-song was corny. Professor Gray produced a pack of cards and, after a while, had collected a group to play poker.

Then Valerie went to the stable to fetch something from her saddle bag, and let out a piercing scream which the hills caught and threw back in an eerie, mocking echo.

"She's seen a ghost," shouted Linda. "She's psychic!"

"It's probably only a rat," remarked Fergie. "I can't understand why girls are frightened of rats. They are such intelligent animals."

Meanwhile Michael Appleby had leapt to his feet and run to Valerie's aid, putting all the other males to shame.

"It's a poor dead dog," he called. "A collie."

Jake was striding towards the stable with Fergie at his heels.

"Ah, it's old Joe's Flossie," he said softly, bending over the corpse. "I'll be damned. A nice merle she was, too." His calm voice was comforting in the darkening stillness of the night. "I'll go down to the farm to let them know. Now just you go back to the fire and we'll boil up some water, and all have a good cup of tea. Scared you, I shouldn't wonder. A lovely bitch she was, but he said she was sick—came up here to die, I suppose, and Joe's getting too old to look far. A shame that is, a damned shame. Well, we must give her a decent burial, mustn't

29

we. There are plenty of teabags along with the provisions, Sandy."

Michael brought Valerie back to the fireside, while Jake strode off with that marvellous spring in his step which, like the lilt in a Welsh voice, is something belonging to the hills and the wild places, which cannot be urbanised even when houses and streets and shops are all around.

Professor Gray went to look at the dead dog, being of a macabre turn of mind, and Eric Small, who had been gloomily attempting to read a book in the firelight, said he thought he would take a walk, and was joined by Helen Wetherall.

"I feel like talking about poetry to someone; we may be kindred spirits," she announced, with a plaintive smile.

I put water on to boil for tea, then picked up a hurricane lantern.

"I'm going to check the ponies. Anyone want to come?"

"Me, me," cried the twins.

"Aren't you scared?" asked Valerie.

"No, I don't mind the dark."

The ponies were not far from the field gate, but all except Mimosa and Silverstar galloped away with their tails up when they saw the lantern. Our ponies, accustomed to nocturnal visits, stayed behind and welcomed us with little whinnies which gave me that nice warm feeling aroused sometimes by a really friendly greeting.

"Oh, aren't they *sweet*!" said Felicity. "I think you and Fergie are terribly lucky."

I found them some oats from my jodhpur pockets, and they nuzzled us, their warm breath silver in the inky darkness. We leant against the gate for a while and talked and petted the ponies, and listened to a nightjar and then an owl sweeping across the sky.

When we got back the water had not reached boiling point. Jake was digging by the light of the other lantern, making a rectangular grave not far from the stable, and Fergie was making a wooden cross out of two pieces of wood he had found somwhere, having managed to extract three nails from a broken fence.

"I do so admire your resourcefulness," said Helen Wetherall, back from her walk.

Suddenly there was a clink, as Jake's fork hit metal.

"Hullo," he said. "What have we here?"

Looking romantic in the lantern light, he straightened his back, then leaned down again and, groping in the darkness of the hole, pulled out a round object, which he wiped clean in damp grass before holding it close to the lantern.

"Something from the old days, I shouldn't wonder," he said.

"A necklace, something to go round a lady's neck," said Helen Wetherall, who had been watching. "I worked in a museum once. What did they call them? Wait a minute while I recall that curious time in my life."

"Is it Roman?" I asked.

"A torc!" cried Helen Wetherall. "That's it, a pre-Roman torc. Jake, it could be very interesting."

Without a word Jake put it in his pocket and continued digging. I understood his feelings. It wasn't that he wasn't interested in the find. It was simply that when there was a job in hand he liked to give it all his attention. The torc would be discussed later when the dog was buried, or the next day when we paused for lunch and there was time to pass it from hand to hand.

I turned away as Valerie came up to me.

"The toilet," she said, anxiously. "I'm afraid to go to

the farm by myself . . . you know . . . read too many ghost stories . . ." She gave a nervous laugh.

"And you haven't a light—I'll come with the lantern, then I *must* make the tea. Come on, but let's find out if there's anyone else who wants to go. Most people are actually going to wash under the tap by the barn. Jake doesn't believe in showers and baths on adventure holidays."

A few moments later several of us set off across the field towards the grey farm which stood silent and unlit as though asleep. The moon had risen behind the shoulder of a hill and sent a shaft of silvery light to help us on our way.

"I wonder whether Jake realises his find could be treasure trove," said Helen Wetherall.

"Jonathan says it could be worth ten thousand pounds if it's genuine," said Valerie.

"Jonathan? How does *he* know about the find?"

"The news had spread like wildfire, didn't you realise?" said Jane. "Well, it's not every day someone digs up a torc, is it? The Professor can't wait to lay his hands on it, and Michael Appleby talks of ringing up a friend in the antique trade."

"Jake had better keep it under lock and key," said Helen Wetherall. "There are going to be a lot of envious eyes and itchy fingers around tomorrow."

CHAPTER THREE

TUESDAY

I wakened as the dawn's thin light gleamed through the cobwebs which all but obscured the old stable window. Sitting up, I loosened the zip of my sleeping bag so I could look around. All night I had slept with it fully closed, with only my nose peeping out, for these were special waterproof bags originally made for the Air Force and suitable for use in all weathers and climates. A few feet away Helen Wetherall lay on her back, snoring gently, and, further on, one of the twins muttered in her sleep.

Presently I dressed and went into the shed next door where the stores had been put. Here I found three large packets of sliced white bread, four boxes of eggs, two jars of marmalade, four slabs of butter and a packet of tea bags. One of the preserving pans had oil in it from the night before, so I took the other one, filled it with water and then started relighting the fire. The night had been dry but the dew had dampened the last of the kindling and it was a while before a golden flame sprang into life.

"Well done," said a voice. "Any chance of a cup of tea?"

Looking round I saw the Professor in pale blue nylon pyjamas and rubber riding boots. His rather fluffy hair was all over the place, his bi-focal glasses perching near the tip of his nose.

"I couldn't sleep—I only need a few hours a night."

"Nor could I," said Igor Polunsky, arriving as if from

33

nowhere. "At least, not peacefully, for I experienced the wildest dreams. I was back in Moscow before the war—it was—how can I say it? Fantastic. The atmosphere! And the snow falling as it only falls in Russia! And yet your Jake was there in his riding things without a hat or coat, a spade in his hand. 'I have come to bury the dead,' he said, and I thought this *is* the revolution. How do you account for that?"

"Too much tea and poker," said the Professor. "Now please tell me, Sandy, when the water's warm, so that I can have a little drop for shaving."

The men went away and I checked the ponies, then Fergie appeared and said that Jake was up and had gone to fetch the milk from the farm.

"We are to fry eggs in the oil left over from last night as soon as four or five people are ready. Meanwhile dole out tea to anyone who wants it. A tin of instant coffee is on the way. Thank goodness, I don't have to shave yet. I saw the Professor ladling out water for himself from the pan, and putting it in an old bucket."

"Jake says he isn't going to bother," I said. "And what's the fun of an adventure holiday if you can't grow a bit of stubble?"

A number of trekkers now started to emerge, holding mugs into which we popped teabags, saying that tea would be ready as soon as Jake got back.

That first morning passed quite well considering how in-experienced everyone was. Most of the trekkers helped with the grooming and we were all mounted and away by nine o'clock. Eric Small asked whether we could have a choice of bread in future, as wholemeal, he said was much more health-giving than white, and Jake said he would see what could be done. The Professor hoped the food would not always be fried, and Helen Wetherall suggested a change of marmalade, "Or," she added, "a little honey might make a welcome choice." Jake, who will eát anything within reason, remarked quietly to me that there were some who would always grumble even if they were served Scotch salmon and strawberries and cream.

Treasure was very fresh and went sideways if she was not in the lead, and Rolo decided that Jonathan was a bore and, shying suddenly, left him in a gorse bush.

"He did that deliberately," said the student, picking prickles from his seat. "He tossed me off as though I was a boring old haversack."

I caught the dun, who was grazing contentedly as though nothing had happened, and refrained from telling Jonathan that he had been sitting like a sack of potatoes, but I looked imploringly at Jake, who said, "Change him."

"With whom?" I glanced desperately at my group, the trousered typists seemed quite at home, their faces pink above chiffon scarves tucked into skin-tight sweaters; and Igor appeared confident on reliable Cadbury.

"Not being averse to prickles, I will volunteer willingly to change," said the Professor. "Danger, in any case, adds spice to life."

"I don't think Sandpiper is quite the mount for this young man, thank you all the same," said Jake. "Mrs. Gray, would you consider . . ."

"I'm a bit old to fall," said the grey-headed woman, nervously adjusting her bowler hat, "and I must say I am very happy with Bournville. We understand each other."

"Look, I'm nervous, but really quite experienced and I think I can manage Rolo, if I'm not made to gallop before I'm ready, so how about Jonathan having Bullfinch?

He's really a very friendly soul," suggested Helen Wetherall, before sliding sedately from her saddle.

"Very good of you, thank you. It seems a good answer. Rolo's a fine pony if you give him a good rein and sit tight," said Jake.

So the big bay, Bullfinch, joined my ride and Rolo was soon trotting just behind the restless Treasure, who was sweating and tossing her lovely head from side to side.

Presently Jake halted at a cottage where he collected fifteen packages of sandwiches and small apple pies for our lunch.

We stopped again by a stream and here at last, sitting on a boulder, Jake took out the torc and inspected it.

"Went round a lady's throat, I suppose," he said. "Looks like brass."

"Can I see?" Helen Wetherall held out a lined hand in which the veins stood out like threads of wool, bilberry-red.

"It's pre-Christian, you know, Iron Age," she said. "But it needs cleaning."

"Iron Age," echoed Kristianne. "That I think is something. I must tell my family when I return home. Can I? Can I just try it round my neck?"

"Too dirty," said Jake, stuffing the torc back into his pocket. "Besides, it probably wouldn't fit round, women's necks were smaller then."

"Yes," said Jonathan, munching a ham sandwich. "Think of Iron Age huts, I mean the height—quite ridiculously low!"

"But I would love, just the feel, to know that I had somehow linked with that unknown lady of all those hundreds of years ago. You understand the thrill . . ."

"Yes," said Jake. "I understand. Perhaps later on, but now it's time to make a move."

Eight of the trekkers galloped that day and even Jonathan enjoyed a canter on steady old Bullfinch, although afterwards he dug in his pockets for a cigarette as though his nerves needed calming.

"Jake, do you have a match? Are we the only smokers here?" he looked disconsolately around. "I feel like a leper."

"So long as you don't smoke at night where there's straw, we are all happy," replied Jake, riding back with a box of matches in his hand. "Here, you strike the match; my mare goes off like a bomb when she hears the noise." He leaned over as he spoke and, at the same time, Treasure shied violently, and he all but fell off.

"Bravo!" cried the Russian. "I had this little feeling that you were *glued* to the saddle, now I know the truth. It is a paste, just so-so," he gesticulated with his hands. "A help, but not quite perfect, for you *nearly* fell."

"Say that again!" said Jake. "Whoa, you silly girl, whoa now!" He ran a hand down the sweating mare's neck.

That evening we came to a deserted cottage used long ago by a shepherd, with a stream beside it. It had four rooms, an outside lavatory and no windows. Here, too, the floors were covered in straw and a pile of food awaited our arrival. There was a huge, round-handled utensil like a coal scuttle full of meat and vegetables.

"Stew tonight," said Jake, "hung above the fire in that cauldron. Very nice, very nice indeed." He rubbed his hands together.

All around us stood the hills, still as stones and muffled here and there by stretches of woodland soft in the greyness of evening. There was not even a whisper of breeze and our voices seemed an intrusion.

"I feel somehow at peace tonight," said Helen

Wetherall, as we turned out the ponies. "It must be all the exercise in the fresh air, but also something about the countryside. You know I *am* enjoying myself."

And I guessed that she was especially pleased that she had been able to manage Rolo. Maybe, I thought, she was one of those rare people who would be always willing to try something new so long as she was able.

The stew took longer to cook than Jake had expected and several of the trekkers grew irritable with hunger.

"Solitude and want are the twin nurses of the soul," said the Russian.

"I don't see any solitude, although just now I could do with some," snapped the Professor, who had become exasperated with the twins who were singing some of the latest pop songs to keep up their spirits.

Fergie and Kristianne had gone for a walk in the woods, taking one of the hurricane lanterns, so there was little hope of playing poker, since Jake needed the other one for checking over saddlery and unpacking the fifteen mousses in white plastic containers which were to be our dessert.

"I think we ought to have some fruit," grumbled Eric Small. "Or why not cheese?"

At last the vegetables and meat in the cauldron were soft enough to serve, and Jake ladled out helpings on to the large dinner plates which had miraculously turned up again with the provisions. Everyone gathered round the fire to eat except for Fergie and the Swedish girl.

"I hope nothing has happened to them," said Helen Wetherall. Jake in reply started to whistle the *Teddy Bears' Picnic*, and, as the delicious stew began to be digested, tempers at once started to improve. Everyone except Eric Small accepted a second helping, and three large packets of bread disappeared with amazing speed.

Then Helen Wetherall said a search party should be sent to look for Fergie and Kristianne. Michael Appleby instantly volunteered to go, and Jonathan said he would accompany him so long as they could have the second hurricane lantern.

"I've always longed to carry one of those things. I shall feel like a coastguard," he said.

"Well, don't fall in the sea," said Jake, who was inclined to leave Fergie and Kristianne to find their own way back.

"Now we have no light," said the Professor.

"Until the moon comes out," said Igor Polunsky.

"Well, you asked for adventure," said Eric Small. "Anyone afraid?" The twins giggled and Linda said, "A little."

"What, a big strong girl like you?" said Mrs. Gray. "These mousses taste like scented soap. Where *did* you find them, Jake?"

"Put some water on for the washing up, will you, Sandy," said Jake, being adept at ignoring criticism.

"We're going to see the ponies in the dark," announced Felicity, and ran off with her sister before anyone had time to stop them.

An hour passed. The twins came back and the moon rose, a lovely wraith in a dark, cloudless sky.

"I love the moon. She is my ideal," said Igor Polunsky. "Delicate, silver and silent. I could gaze upon her all night."

"And dead," said the Professor.

"What did you say?"

"The moon is dead. We need a bottle of wine. It's getting cold."

Jake threw more wood on the fire.

"The advertisement said *Sleep under the stars* and I'm going to do just that. The cottage is damp and melancholy.

39

It speaks of old age and dust," said the Russian. "So." He went away, came back with his sleeping bag and, still wearing breeches, long socks and a high-necked dark blue sweater, slipped inside. "There now," he said, zipping the bag up to his nose. "The fire will keep away the wolves. Good night, ladies and gentlemen."

"Do you think we could have a little coffee?" asked Eric Small, in a slightly pained voice. "I'm not going to bed while those youngsters are lost." He shot an angry glance in the Russian's direction.

"I'll tell you what, I'll put the water on and give you the tin, and you make yourself a cup when you're ready," said Jake. "Meanwhile it looks as though another search party must go out. Sandy, you don't mind the night do you? Will you come with me?"

"Of course," I said.

"Count on me, Jake, if you need assistance," said Helen Wetherall, "I may be getting old, but I've got a lot of common sense."

"Thank you."

The Professor cleared his throat.

"No," cried his wife. "No, Geoffrey, your sight is too bad."

"There must be a monster in the woods devouring everybody. Do you think you'll come back?" asked Valerie with a shudder. "I'm scared!"

"Nothing more dangerous than the odd fox or badger," said Jake. "Come on, Sandy, I know you're game."

The woods *were* very dark, being mainly made up of firs, but here and there the moonlight sent slanting beams of silver which showed us the way. Every now and then we called, "Fergie, Kristianne!" and our voices seemed light and useless in the greatness of the night.

"There aren't bogs, are there?"

"No, of course not, Sandy. Woods like these never have bogs."

"There couldn't be a maniac, could there?"

"Why should he land up here of all places?"

"An escaped bull?"

"He might injure one, but not two."

"Or four?" I said, feeling increasingly nervous.

Now and then leaves and twigs moved as birds shifted at the sound of our approach and each time this happened my heart missed a beat.

"Fergie, Kristianne, where are you? Jonathan, Michael!"

There could be some quite simple explanation. There always is, I told myself.

"That Swedish girl's a rare one, isn't she?" said Jake.

"I suppose so," I replied doubtfully, not knowing what he meant.

"Probably find them all sitting down and playing poker," said Jake.

"But they were hungry."

A fox ran across our path, thin and reddish-brown with a fine bushy tail, and rabbits scuttled into burrows, and every twig we broke sounded like the report from a gun.

At last we saw a gleam of light, yellow through the tree trunks, and heard an answering cry of "Here, help, here. She's trapped!"

"Fergie," I said.

"Yes, I'd know that Scottish roll to an 'r' anywhere," said Jake. "Coming. Hold on. Coming!"

The light grew brighter, yellower and more welcoming as we drew near, the snapping twigs became unimportant, and, all at once, the moon rose higher sending a great shaft of light into the very depths of the wood. And then we saw them. Kristianne curled up in a strange position

41

on the ground and Fergie standing awkwardly at her side.

"What happened? For goodness sake what happened?"

"Look," said Fergie. "Poor Kristianne tripped and fell and see how her foot is trapped."

And sure enough there was her foot firmly held between two boulders.

"But if it got in, it will come out," said Jake calmly.

"But it hurts terribly. I've tried pulling and the pain was too great. She couldn't stand it, and she didn't want to be left alone." Fergie sounded desperate.

"I nearly fainted right away and I do not like these dark English woods," said Kristianne, turning her pale face towards Jake so that her vivid eyes, moist with anguish, seemed to plead with him.

"Won't the boulders move?"

"I tried that, Jake."

"But, with two of us . . ."

They tried together while I held the hurricane lamp, but the lower boulder was as firm as a rock and the upper one would only move in one direction, nearer to the Swedish girl's foot.

"There's only one thing to do," said Jake. "This." He took the girl's leg and yanked, and at the same moment a piercing scream came from her throat and rent the air with blood-curdling intensity. There was a sudden flap of wings as birds took off from their perches and my own heart seemed to take a leap and then pound my ribs, while the lantern swung wildly for a moment in my right hand.

"Sometimes you must be cruel to be kind," said Jake. "Any bones broken?"

He held her foot in his hands. She was wearing plimsolls. Not ordinary ones, but a pair made of denim with beautiful embroidery. Her face was pale as paper and a couple of tears ran down her cheeks before she shook her head.

"I am sorry. I am quite all right. I thank you." She took her foot away and rubbed her ankle. "It's only sore, no more."

She limped a little, leaning on Fergie as we made our way back through the wood calling, "Jonathan, Michael, where are you?"

Fergie patted me on the back. "I'm sorry," he said. "I'm sorry, Jake, I was feeble."

"No, no, it was my fault. I would not let . . ." Kristianne's voice trailed away.

"Only one reproach," said Jake firmly. "Don't go off again with the lantern. There are fifteen people and two lanterns, Fergie, and it's not right that two people should have one of them to themselves. And we needed your help with the meal."

"I'm sorry," said Fergie. "I really am, Jake."

"My fault, I asked him. I was so bored and the old people were so cross. I couldn't stand it any longer. That professor and Eric . . . they . . . how do you say it?"

"Got on your nerves . . ." I suggested.

"Right."

As we drew near the fire we saw that it was surrounded by little humps, and two standing figures. Eight of the trekkers had decided to sleep like the Russian and the two standing were Jonathan and Michael.

"Oh, you've got them," said Michael.

"And what happened to the search party?" asked Jake, sounding a little caustic.

"Lamp went out," said Jonathan, "no matches to light it with and we were soon hopelessly lost. We went round

43

in circles until suddenly the moon rose and we could see the gate by the ponies' field."

"It shouldn't have gone out, plenty of paraffin," said Jake.

"Well, um, I dropped it," admitted the student.

"I see, well we all know accidents do happen. Now we must get some stew heated up for these poor starving people. Sandy . . ."

"Yes," I called, dashing to find the cauldron.

"All's well that ends well," said Mrs. Gray, sitting up and looking very strange with just her nose peeping out of her grey sleeping bag. "That Russian is snoring. Can someone prod him."

CHAPTER FOUR

WEDNESDAY

The next morning started well. I scrambled three dozen eggs and Michael Appleby toasted sliced bread, on two long toasting forks, and Jane buttered it. Everyone seemed happy with this breakfast, and the Professor, having decided to grow a beard after all, was especially merry.

We left the plates and cutlery for the 'fairies', swilled out our cups in the stream and put them in our saddle bags. Eric Small said he had an embarrassing problem, but no one dared to ask him to explain himself, so we went to catch the ponies with it unsolved.

Mimosa and Silverstar whinnied, as they came across the field like welcoming angels, and I felt proud of them both. As usual, we tied baling string to the fence in appropriate places, to which we attached the ponies, ensuring that the string and not their headcollars would break if they suddenly pulled back. Each mount had a small feed while being groomed. The trekkers were not asked to help, but most of them did, chatting while they worked.

Today Mrs. Wetherall set out across the field calling "Rolo, Rolo, come along, darling," swinging the headcollar in her hand. Rolo watched her with knowing eyes, his lean dun head hanging down and one hind leg resting. He was an individual, unaffected by the behaviour of the other ponies, most of whom were already caught. As Mrs. Wetherall came within a few yards of him, he put his ears back, swung round and made off in the opposite direction.

"Now, now, darling, don't be naughty. Come to your Aunty Helen, come to mother," said the widow.

"That sort of talk makes me sick," muttered Jonathan, still riled that the dun had tossed him into a gorse bush.

"Darling, don't look so cross, it's only me, your Aunty Helen," continued Mrs. Wetherall, and so a pattern was set. The cunning Rolo would wait and watch until she was within a yard of him and then he would be away again.

By the time the rest of us had tacked up, Jake's patience was at an end.

"Come on, Mrs. Wetherall, give that headcollar to me." He strode across the field, but Rolo was not to be deterred. He treated his master exactly as he had treated the widow.

"And the trouble is," Jake remarked on his return, "the artful old devil won't care a damn even if we take the other ponies off. He won't even neigh—he's that independent."

"So what do we do now?" asked Michael Appleby.

"Some of us mount and drive him down here to the gate and hem him in—Sandy, Fergie?"

"Right."

"Cowboy stuff, count on me," said the Professor.

"And us," chorused Jane and Felicity.

"I don't know why Jake keeps a brute like that," said Jonathan, his blue eyes looking cold as steel. "He's a dead loss, if you ask me."

We fanned out: The twins on Crunchie and Peppermint, Michael on Candyfloss, the Professor on Sandpiper, and, a moment later, Kristianne on the lovely Caramelo.

Rolo watched us coolly.

"I've always wanted to do this," said the Professor. "A round-up. Come on, let's move!"

With a little whoop he galloped round behind the dun.

"That little man is so young, so juvenile for his years. It is strange," remarked Kristianne, before urging her mount into an elegant collected canter. But Rolo simply stayed where he was, the prematurely deep hollows above his eyes giving him a learned look.

"He's packed it in," said Jake. "He's not going to join in the game."

"How very unsporting," said the Professor. "I hoped for a rodeo. I'll challenge you to a race today, Michael. Are you game?"

"Yes, but let's sort this out first or we shall be a pony short."

The Professor beat his boots with his whip and made cowboy noises. Michael waved his arms as though he was trying to drive a herd of bullocks, and Jake dismounted.

"Come on, old fellow."

He walked up to the dun gelding, and, talking softly, slipped on the headcollar.

"A wise old devil. He's not going to gallop for nothing," he said.

"And who says horses haven't got brains?" asked Mrs. Wetherall a few moments later. "Now off with the mud, you naughty crafty little monkey."

I helped her groom Rolo, while Jake brought out his torc again and looked at it, rubbing at the dirt with his fingers.

"Do you reckon it's treasure trove, Mrs. Wetherall? Can I keep it or will the Government take it?"

"That I can't say, Jake. But I can write later to tell you whom to ask, or I can make enquiries on your behalf after our lovely adventure is over."

Half an hour later we were on our way with a drizzle of rain falling like dew on our faces and slate-grey clouds chasing each other across an ashen sky.

Jake started to whistle, partly to quieten his mare and partly, I suspect, because he felt low-spirited, this being his way of lifting himself out of any depression.

The groups now began to get a little mixed and I found Michael Appleby riding beside me.

"That Jonathan is something of a nutcase," he told me. "Nattering on about a survival course next year and he couldn't even hold a lantern. Do you know he says Jake's torc is valuable, really valuable, not worth a hundred pounds, but a thousand. He says it's gold, but if the old man likes to think it's brass, so be it."

"He's not an old man," I said crossly.

"Well, not relatively. I mean the Grays are older, but he's in his forties, isn't he?"

"I've never thought," I said. "He can still run and ride, and move hundredweight sacks as though they are three pounds of flour."

"Ah, that's the work he does, isn't it? It keeps him fit."

"I think he's great," cut in Linda, quietly. "He's a real character, like somebody out of a book, *different*."

"I would like him as my dad," said Valerie. "I really would. My own father's lovely, but so *weak*, and Mum's the boss."

"Girls and their fathers, a very different subject," said the Professor, catching up. "You need to be forty before you can understand your parents."

We were climbing up towards a misty sky which told us rain was falling relentlessly on the hilltops; a few sheep bleated at us, lichen clung to boulders, and ragged rowans, sad as scarecrows, grew from the stoniest ground.

"Very bleak," said the Professor.

"But majestic," added Igor. "A certain beauty in its barrenness."

We could see a forsaken cottage growing larger as we came to it through the mist, its empty windows gaping like gaps in a mouth after teeth have been extracted.

"We are not going to be asked to sleep there, are we?" cried Mrs. Gray.

"No," laughed Jake. "But if I'm not mistaken our lunches will be waiting for us inside."

He pushed Treasure forward.

"Come on there! Come on!"

A path with little boulders either side led to the empty doorway and then turned right to meander to the remains of a sheep pen. Through the mist we could feel little gusts of wind like steam from a boiling kettle, only cold. Mrs. Gray's cheeks looked very red; grey wisps of straggly hair had escaped from under her black bowler hat and hung like torn tassels on either side of her face. "Ugh," she said. "Just ugh!" I didn't know whether she was referring to the cottage or the weather.

"Sandwiches again today, but brown, and bananas for dessert to please Mr. Small," announced Jake, and at almost the same moment there was a flutter of wings and a weird squawk followed simultaneously by a terrified equine snort, a scraping and a scrambling noise as Treasure, who had leapt sideways, tried to gain a grip on the slippery boulders. She failed and the next second we saw the bright silver of her shoes as she lay kicking on the ground.

"Jake, are you all right?" Fergie's voice sounded remarkably calm.

The mare righted herself and stood shaking from head to foot.

"Oh dear, oh dear," squeaked Linda. "He's not underneath, is he?"

My brother jumped off Mimosa and took Treasure by the reins, and a moment later I was on the ground too, and Michael Appleby and presently Mrs. Wetherall, who said, in her quiet authoritative way, "My dear, I know a little about first aid."

"Jake?" said Fergie.

He pulled himself up on to a boulder. "Well, that was a bit of a show, wasn't it?" he said.

"He must be made of india rubber," muttered the Professor.

"Let's look you over," said Mrs. Wetherall, putting on a medical voice. "Any bones broken? Your colour's not too good."

"Pain in my leg—something terrible," said Jake. "Anyone got a match?" He fumbled for a cigarette.

"Here." Jonathan threw a packet.

Jake's face had changed. It suddenly looked gaunt, like a rock or piece of sculpture, and his hand shook as he tried to strike a match. Fergie lit a cigarette for him.

"It was a bird, wasn't it," said my brother. "It came out suddenly and frightened Treasure. Any horse would have shied."

"But wasn't she quick, like a flash? So sudden I hadn't a chance."

"What now?" asked the Russian. "Is he hurt, or isn't he?"

"You can't stand, can you?" said Mrs. Wetherall. "Come on, Jake, try." She gave her kind plaintive smile, her eyes warm in her pale, lined face.

He moved and, grimacing, tried to stand, and then sat down again. I came closer as Mrs. Wetherall gently felt his left leg through his breeches and black rubber riding boots.

"I think you have a fracture, Jake," she said, and still smiling looked deep into his face as though to encourage him.

Jonathan swore under his breath. "That just about mucks everything up," he said

"His leg is broken, ya?" asked the Swedish girl. "Well, that is serious. What do we do now?"

"Fifty dollar question," said Michael. "Where's the nearest phone box?"

"Two or three miles up on the top road," said Jake.

"And the nearest farm?" asked the Professor, goggling a little behind his glasses.

"A mile or two down in the valley or half a mile on from the call box," said Jake. "There's Jim Jones down there. He's not a friendly sort, but he'd oblige in an emergency, and I know I can't walk or ride."

"These things always happen in the worst places. Here we are cut off from humanity," began the Russian.

"Oh, stow it," said Jonathan, dismounting. "At least we are not on a mountain."

"Who's going for help?" asked Mrs. Wetherall.

"Fergie," said Jake. "Fergie, go to the farm and explain. Jones can get a tractor or his broken-down old car half-way up, and then they can put me on a hurdle, and if they've got a drop of brandy, bring it up."

"No, no," said Mrs. Wetherall. "Supposing you need an anaesthetic?"

"That can wait," said Jake. "I need something for shock, else I'll be shivering like a frightened dog in half an hour."

"I could cut off your boot and have a closer look," suggested Mrs. Wetherall.

"No, thanks, they cost me a mint of money and I don't want them spoilt," said Jake.

Fergie handed me Treasure, mounted Silverstar and set off down the hill. The sky darkened. The bay mare yanked at my arms and Mimosa nibbled at tufts of heather.

"You're a daft lot, all standing around. Why don't you put the headcollars on your ponies, tie them up and have the sandwiches?" asked Jake. "Come on, Mr. Polunsky and you girls, your ponies' backs could do with a rest."

Jane gave Felicity Peppermint's reins and went into the cottage with Michael Appleby to find the food, while the rest of us started to follow Jake's instructions.

"Does this mean the end of the adventure?" asked Valerie with a grim little smile.

"I don't know."

Jake's providers had done well this time. There were fifteen packets of tongue and lettuce and cheese and tomato sandwiches, and thirty bananas and a Dundee cake in a tin.

"None for you," said Mrs. Wetherall, looking at her patient. "They will have to give you an anaesthetic to set the bones, and that must be done on an empty stomach."

"I'll have his," said Jonathan. "I'm starving."

Eating, we all felt better.

"We can carry on, can't we?" asked Felicity. "I mean we are all more or less grown-up, and you and Fergie can show us the way."

"I don't know."

"I felt at sea, realising that we had never discussed the route with Jake, who always travelled without a map, finding his way by natural landmarks, trees, strange formations of rock and the contours of the hills.

"We can't stop now, Sandy," argued Felicity. *"Please."*

"I'm not the boss. You must talk to Jake."

Jake's face was like the mist, grey and damp, with his blue eyes pale as pebbles, and his voice had slowed down. There was no doubt that he was suffering from shock.

"Here," the Russian took off his coat and laid it over the injured man's knees. "It's all right, I don't feel the cold. You must be kept warm." He looked at his watch, a large dialed affair on a wide strap round his hairy wrist.

"Half an hour since Fergie left. How long will he be?"

"He has to go slowly at first where the ground is rough, but he can canter the last bit."

"Where are we heading for, Jake?" asked the Professor. "I mean, what are the plans now?"

"Up to you, isn't it? You can carry on with Fergie and Sandy as your guides or you can pack it in this afternoon and I'll refund part of what you paid me. I'm sorry to let you down like this. It's a funny situation when the most experienced man meets with the accident rather than a beginner, but it's happened and we've all got to make the best of it."

"The ball is in our court, then," said the Professor. "Shall we take a vote?"

"There's an old scout motto," began Michael.

"Oh, stuff it, the boy scouts are out of date," cut in Jonathan.

"Now then, you boys!" said Mrs. Gray. "I think it's going to be a risk without our leader."

"But, dear, that's what we're here for, an adventure. Are you suggesting we can't read maps and look after ourselves?"

"Is there a map, Geoffrey? I think the whole trip has been planned by instinct."

"I say 'never say die'," put in Helen Wetherall. "We are

not going to be beaten by a tiresome accident. Surely we have more backbone than that?"

The grown-ups argued for a while and then at the Professor's suggestion took a vote, and decided unanimously to carry on with the ride.

"And you and Fergie must be the equitation experts," said Helen Wetherall.

Realising I was expected to be efficient, I shook myself out of a reverie.

"I need pencil and paper, so that Jake can write down our ports of call."

"I love your romantic language," said the Russian, smiling through his beard. "Anyone else would have said stopping places but you make us see ships and a sea and much bustle. It's wonderful."

Jake wrote down a list of names and places and vague directions. Then we heard voices, and two strong men came over the hill, looming out of the mist like people from another age.

"Where's the casualty? Ar, 'ere, 'ad a fall then, Jake?" They carried a hurdle and two blankets.

Jake joked: "Not brought me any brandy then?"

"Brandy? No one said anything about brandy. Come on then, mate. Got to lift you, 'ave we? Not much of a weight, are you? All that riding keeps you slim, don't it?"

"Ah, but look at those muscles!"

With much backchat and chaffing, the two labourers heaved Jake with surprising tenderness on to the hurdle.

"He can keep my coat," announced Igor Polunsky. "I should be honoured."

"A pillow for his head, half a mo," cried Helen Wetherall, digging in one of her saddlebags. "Here," she handed the men a towel, "use that."

"Anyone know what happened to Fergie?" I asked.

"The boy? He rode off to a telephone, said he wanted a doctor at the farm. The Jones 'ave gone to Ludlow. There was only us two around," replied the burliest of the men.

"Had he money?" asked Michael.

"Yes, he always has tuppence in his pocket. He expects disasters these days," I said.

"Well then, off we go, give us Jake's horse. We'll take her down at the same time."

"Good luck," I said.

Jake looked very small on the hurdle, a body made only of sinew and bone and muscle, but very much alive. He raised a hand in salute.

"Take care, Sandy," he said. "Don't put too much on your own shoulders. Have a good trek, everyone. Not too much galloping, professor, and watch those cigarettes, Jonathan." He gave his quizzical smile, and then a grimace of pain, and then he was out of sight as the men carried him down the hill.

"An extraordinary character," remarked Eric Small. "The ride won't be the same without him."

We grazed the ponies until Fergie returned.

"I've rung Dad," he told me "He's seeing about the doctor and he's dropping round to Jake's wife. He'll see about things."

"Oh, great," I said. "Well, now I suppose we ought to get going again."

We rebridled the ponies and continued on our way. Jake's directions seemed muddling but were actually excellent. We found the twisted ash, the barrel holly, the broken three-quarter gate and the track that led to the village which he had listed without trouble, and stopped at the café to collect steaming coffee in cartons.

"Expected you an hour ago," the waitress said. "Do you want some biscuits, too?—they're only plain."

"A little sustenance will be very welcome," answered Eric Small. "I think we are all suffering a trifle from shock."

By this time everyone was much firmer in the saddle, so after the coffee we all enjoyed a brisk canter up a long hill, and then started our descent down towards a valley where a dark wood threaded through the landscape like braid in a green taffeta dress. Michael Appleby whistled a jaunty tune.

The Russian brought his mount to a halt. "Let us pause a while. Such a view is like nectar to the soul!" he said. "See how the shadows lie."

"Where are we sleeping tonight, Sandy?" asked Mrs. Gray, looking matter-of-fact and old-fashioned in her bowler and widely-cut breeches.

"I'm not sure. Jake said a stable and a cottage, miles from anywhere. It's the other side of that wood."

"Don't you know the name of the place?"

"Yes, but although we are still just in England, it's got an unpronounceable Welsh name."

Fergie came up beside me. "Look out," he said. "Watch Fudge!"

The liver chestnut was indeed taking hold and rushing forward down the hill as though a bucket of oats would meet her at the bottom. And white-faced Linda was hanging on to the mane and doing nothing.

"Kris!" shouted Fergie.

The Swedish girl swung round and, sizing up the situation in a moment, grabbed Fudge's reins and brought her to a halt.

"She's great, isn't she?" said my brother. "But . . ."

"But what?"

"Oh, nothing."

We reached our destination at six o'clock and found the usual sacks of feed and boxes of food awaiting us.

"Ah, chicken portions. Great! *And* a grid. I'll be cook tonight. Any volunteer helpers?" asked Michael.

"Us," replied Jane. "Felicity and me."

"And I'll look after the drink," volunteered Jonathan.

"I'll light the fire. I love kindling flames, it attracts the primitive element in me," said the Professor.

"I'll help Fergie with the ponies," announced Kristianne.

"No surprise there," said Linda.

We missed Jake, and yet it was a merry evening, for the trekkers were like school children when all the teachers are away sick, and it was lovely not to have to cook. The chicken was a little burnt here and there but eaten with fresh rolls, butter, tomatoes and cress it tasted delicious. The rain had gone and the clouds lightened, and now and then we caught a glimpse of the moon. The fairies had left a huge round cheese and two tins of crisp salty biscuits and another jar of instant coffee.

"Do we sleep in or out tonight?" asked Igor at ten o'clock.

"Well, the usual beds of straw await us," said Eric Small. "I think Jake really thinks we are cattle."

"It's the stars for me," said the Professor.

"Listen," said Fergie, moving away from Kristianne who had been leaning against him. "A car."

"Who's there?" called Helen Wetherall.

There were headlights shining through a band of trees, then the sound of a car door shutting, followed by silence.

"Spooky, very spooky," said Valerie.

"Look, a torch. Someone's coming." Linda sounded frightened.

The Russian got to his feet. Michael Appleby flexed his muscles. But it was only Dad.

"Came to see if you were all right," he said. "And brought a couple of maps and a list of the stopping places. Jake's leg *is* fractured, but too swollen to be put in plaster straight away. They may decide to pin it. The specialist will have a look tomorrow."

Dad looked very big. He seemed to ooze self-confidence. He chatted to Michael Appleby and my brother for a while and then he said: "I've brought a bit of cash, Fergie, in case it's needed. Don't hesitate to ring. Oh, and by the way, I have to announce that there's one mishap which has upset Jake—he's lost that gold necklet or what-have-you."

"The torc! Oh, not the torc!" cried Helen Wetherall.

"Yes, the torc. He told me where the accident happened and I went there just before dark and searched exactly where he fell, but there was nothing there."

"It was a find of historic importance," said Helen Wetherall.

"Worth a few hundred pounds," put in Jonathan.

"And so *beautiful*," added Kristianne.

"Is he very cut up?" asked Fergie.

"Well, you know Jake doesn't really show his feelings, but he's certainly disappointed."

"Life is cruel," said the Russian. "Now if you will excuse me, I'm going to clean my teeth."

"And I must be back, got to meet someone off the last train. Good luck then." Dad strode away, leaving me with a sudden gust of home sickness.

"Give our love to Mummy and Leary and to the pussy-cat," I called.

"Perhaps someone picked it up, the torc I mean—the labourers or . . ." Michael Appleby looked at us all.

"You sound like the first page of a thriller," said the Professor, waving his arms in the air. "Page two will see a ghastly murder."

CHAPTER FIVE

THURSDAY

I was dreaming of home. Leary was chasing Mummy's hens and someone was screaming. I opened my eyes, expecting to see the door of my bedroom, the patterned green wallpaper and rush-seated chair, instead there was inky darkness, the cold night air and the thumping of my heart. Where was I? The trek! Out of doors, by the fire which had gone out. I struggled with the zip of my sleeping bag. There were other voices now, people moving through the darkness. The terrible screaming had stopped.

"Light a lantern." It was Michael's voice.

"In the cottage, someone in the cottage," cried Fergie.

I was up and running. The cottage loomed like a broken hill, the door swinging madly in the wind. Was it murder?

"It's Valerie! What is it, a ghost? Speak, speak!"

"Where are the matches?"

"The girl is hysterical, slap her face."

A light flared in the darkness, showing me Fergie with a lantern. I went into the cottage, which smelt of damp stones and old bones and dust. Now the yellow glow from the lantern threw patterns on the walls. I was frightened; when I paused my knees actually knocked together. Valerie's weak little face was chalk white, her poor protruding teeth chattered.

Michael Appleby's left arm was round her shoulders. Fergie leaned over her, his lean, chiselled face creased with anxiety. Linda hovered in the background.

"An animal in my hair, a bat!"

"A bat? Was that all?" Fergie's voice was incredulous. "But they are little harmless things."

"But in my hair. I am sorry, I was frightened."

"Only sort of mice with wings," went on my brother.

"But mice, mice, mice by my bed would make *me* scream," said Linda. "And Fergie, don't be cruel. Bats get tangled in hair and you can't get them out."

She ran a hand nervously through her own dark brown locks, which came down below her shoulders. She was wearing shiny pyjamas patterned in a Japanese style, which I suddenly coveted for myself.

"But you woke us all for a bat, a harmless little creature," began Fergie again in a tone of pained reproach. "They have a marvellous radar system and don't bump into things. The hair business is an old wives' tale."

"Now, now, old man, where's your imagination— chivalry, I might even say? Women have been terrified of bats, mice and rats for centuries, and many men, too." The librarian was standing in the doorway, holding tightly to the trousers of his striped wincyette pyjamas. "I am sorry to be the last young male to come to the rescue, but you see my elastic has perished," he smiled, and then suddenly his face paled and with a strange squeak he leapt sideways, as a little brown mouse ran across the floor with a bit of bread in its mouth. At the same time he let go of his pyjamas, and, as they slipped, he let out a horrified hiss and bounded from the cottage into the kindly dark.

Linda giggled. "It's an adventure holiday all right. I don't know what I expected but certainly nothing like this. Oh, Val, wasn't that great, the trousers and the mouse."

She broke into great gusts of laughter.

"Now what is the joke?" The librarian was back, his trousers up again and firmly grasped. "My goodness, a mouse, did you see? It gave me quite a little turn. They carry fleas you know."

"Some humans do, too," remarked Fergie.

"Sandy," said Michael, "will you help me get the fire going and make tea for all these shaken people. If only I were in touch with Jake's mysterious fairies I would order a kettle forthwith. These primitive cauldrons are all very well when there are no emergencies or nervous break-downs."

"A mouse," shouted Valerie. "Listen, scratching behind that wall. I'm not going to stay a moment longer in this lousy cottage."

"No, that's right," said Fergie. "Come outside and relax in the fresh air. There's a brilliant breeze blowing from Wales."

Plenty of wood had been left for us and, as the fire crackled and hissed into life, the dawn spread miraculously across the eastern sky, and the first cocks began to herald another day. The older people slept on and also Jonathan, the twins and Kristianne.

Meanwhile, Valerie and Linda huddled together like orphans in a storm, the tips of their noses red as cherries.

"Who do you think took the torc?" asked Fergie over a cup of tea.

"*Took* it?"

All of the trekkers except Michael were out of earshot.

"Yes, Sandy, *took* it."

I rubbed my hands across my eyes and tried to direct my thoughts to the problem.

"Your brother and I reckoned someone picked it up after the accident, while we were grazing the ponies and waiting for the rescue party," Michael explained. "You see, before he broke his leg Jake was looking after it very carefully and apparently he told your father that he had no recollection of feeling it in his pocket as he was carried down to the farm."

"But who would want it?"

"Lots of people," said Fergie.

"But the trekkers are all such friendly people."

"Jonathan?" asked Michael.

"There's no harm in him," I replied.

"The Professor?"

"But he's an important person, I mean . . ."

"An academic, but there *are* bad academics," said Fergie.

"Polunsky is an unknown quantity," suggested Michael, "and I never trust a foreigner."

"Oh, what an awful thing to say." I was really annoyed.

"Well, let's agree to keep our eyes open," said Fergie. "Maybe we are wrong. Dad's going back to search again, right down to the farm. Look, people are waking. A cup of tea, Mr. Polunsky?"

"I think Igor would be better."

The Russian stepped out of his sleeping bag. As usual he was still wearing his breeches and socks and a dark blue sweater. I wondered whether he had forgotten to bring pyjamas.

It was a wonderful morning and the cameraderie of the evening before was still with us as we cooked breakfast under a sky as soft as liquid lead. The air had that damp quality that you only find in Britain and the grass sparkled in the dew.

All the trekkers tacked up their own ponies and we were away by half-past nine, with Michael Appleby acting as map reader.

"I'm going into the army, so I might as well put in plenty of practice," he told us.

"Brave boy, I wish I had a soldier son," said Mrs. Wetherall, before reciting three war poems by an obscure poet called May Wedderburn Cannan.

"I can't bear people who romanticise war," declared Jonathan, who had clearly taken a dislike to the widow.

"What about food?" asked Eric Small, as we turned off down a muddy lane that led between tall hazel hedges.

"Lunch, you mean? That's fixed up at a bed and breakfast place." I consulted Jake's list as I spoke.

"And it's my job to get you there," said Michael, as though he was enjoying the responsibility.

Kristianne rode beside Fergie, smiling up into his face as she talked.

"The lovely Swede is smitten with your brother," said the Professor, catching up with me.

"Now don't be silly, Geoffrey," snapped his wife. "They are far too young to be thinking of that sort of thing."

"Not nowadays," said the Professor.

"Halt, please!" cried Michael. "Wait a minute, yes, yes, here we branch off down into the valley—single file now, the path is narrow."

"Is he going to be a bossy boots?" asked Linda. "Remember, Sandy, you and Fergie are in charge."

"Only of the horses," I replied, laughing. "I wouldn't like to be in charge of the humans, thank you."

We came to the bed and breakfast place at noon and, banging on the wide chocolate-brown door of the farmhouse, I felt a sense of triumph. A thin, worried looking woman opened it.

"Oh, you must be Jake's trekkers then," she said. "I've been wondering, you see, knowing about the accident. I thought you might not make it. Now what would you like? I've not cut anything yet."

"Chicken sandwiches, please," I replied promptly for

that was what I wanted most at that particular moment. Indeed I was so hungry that my mouth began to water at the thought.

"Haven't got any chicken handy, not just now."

"Tongue?"

"I've a tin, but not enough for a dozen riders."

"Beef?"

"Sorry, there's a lot of you, and I didn't take anything out of the freezer because I thought with Jake laid up and all . . ." her voice trailed away, the lines between her brows deepened with anxiety. She had a little dark face, all skin and bone.

"Well, what *do* you have?"

"Eggs."

"Any cress?"

"No, sorry."

I imagined Eric Small's remarks if served a meal without vitamin C.

"I've sliced bread, I took it out last night before I heard the news, that's one mercy."

"Well, we are *awfully* hungry. Look, could you make us a great jug of coffee and a pot of tea, and give us a bottle of milk and a bowl of sugar? We've got plastic cups, and then if we can turn the horses loose in your yard, we can revive ourselves while you make up your mind what to give us to eat."

I spoke quickly because I could see Eric Small and Mrs. Gray advancing on me down the garden path, and neither looked in a pleasant mood. Like lions they were dangerous when hungry.

"All right then, I'll do my best, you can be sure of that."

The situation was saved, and soon the ponies were

65

wandering in the yard, pulling at hay stacked in a Dutch barn and drinking from a trough. The coffee and tea came and then, half an hour later, a meat tin piled high in sandwiches, a dozen rounds of ham, and half a dozen each of corned beef and tongue and the rest egg and tomato.

"What is there for sweet?" asked Eric Small, looking aggressive.

"Ice cream," said the worried woman. "That's a stand-by in our job, strawberry or vanilla?"

Revived at last, good-tempered again and inclined to joke, we rode off once more at two o'clock, just as the sky darkened and the first drops of rain started to fall. Before us a great shoulder of hill stood shrouded in mist and from its slopes came a south-west wind blowing directly in our faces.

"The rain's coming our way," said Igor. "See it coming with the mist; feel the heaviness of the sky, how it weighs down on us! I'm glad Jake didn't keep my coat. To be wet and hungry is terrible, to be wet and fed, well, that is not so bad. Would you not agree, Professor?"

"Oh, a full stomach always helps, no doubt about that, and those tongue sandwiches were delicious."

I glanced at Fergie with a wry smile, for the Professor, Igor and Jonathan had wolfed all the tongue and corned beef sandwiches before anyone else had had the chance to try them.

We rode through a valley turned up away from the hill, so that when the storm broke the rain hit us on the right-hand side, driving our ponies to walk like crabs, their poor heads bent and their ears flattened in misery. Fergie and I had riding macs, but the rest of the trekkers had brought only little plastic coats or anoraks which did little to protect their thighs and knees.

"We must shelter," shouted Michael above the roaring of the wind.

"Down there," called Igor. "See by the stream, there are trees."

"Only rowans," shouted the Professor. "Too small."

We started to trot.

"Help," shouted Linda. "Stop, stop! Toffee!"

And the next minute the little dun came cantering by with her head between her legs, determined to find shelter somewhere, Fudge followed, and then Crunchie and Peppermint, and a moment later the Professor on Sandpiper. Away they went down a narrow path with the rain pounding them and the mud flying all around.

"Fergie, what shall we do?" Suddenly I felt desperate.

"Nothing, we can't get ahead of them and if we follow we shall only make the ponies increase their speed. We must continue on our way and pick up the pieces."

"Dear Fergie, always the strong decisive man," said Kristianne.

We found Linda first, sitting in a pool of water, weeping, her teeth chattering with cold.

"I can't get up. I can't move."

"Where's the pain?" asked Fergie.

"Pain?"

"Do you hurt anywhere?"

"Hurt?"

Oh heavens! I thought, she's concussed or perhaps her skull is cracked. I felt terribly responsible. Could I not have caught her reins as she galloped by?

"Hysteria. She's all right," said Helen Wetherall, sliding from her saddle. "Come on, my girl, up!"

She took both of Linda's small pale hands and pulled, and in a trice the pathetic shivering girl was on her feet.

"Now a towel."

"Here." Michael was first, with rather a nasty cheap striped one, with which the widow started to rub the girl's hands and face with great vigour like a groom rubbing down a wet horse.

"We must get the circulation going, ducky," she said. "Now chin up, my dear. I've seen people acting like this in the blitz, but a fall from a pony is nothing. Come on, pull yourself together."

"She sounds like a school teacher at my primary school," said Jonathan.

"But she talks sense," said Igor. "She is a genius, so frail but so determined. She is indefatigable, an example to all of us and, if I may say so, a truly English woman."

"I'll go on and find the others," shouted Fergie, urging a bedraggled Silverstar forward.

"Now, dear, up you get," said Helen Wetherall. "You should always remount immediately after a fall otherwise you might lose your nerve."

"I never want to ride again nor to come out in this horrible countryside. I hate it all, and I wish I had never come."

"Oh dear, spoiled child syndrome," muttered Jonathan.

"Come on," said Michael. "Haven't you been in the Girl Guides?"

"No, I have *not*," retorted Linda, with such force that we knew she was better. Then she put a foot in the stirrup and we realised the crisis was over, at least for the moment.

The Professor came back, soaking wet but smiling.

"Mission completed," he said.

"What do you mean?" asked his wife.

"We've found a copse, great chestnut trees."

"You mean you *meant* to gallop off like that?" I asked.

"Yes, of course. Didn't the rest of them? Sometimes a

man of action is needed. The others are sheltering. I came back to tell you."

"Words fail me, Geoffrey, and this poor girl was thrown," said his wife.

"Well, let's get to the copse," said Michael. "For heaven's sake, I'm soaked."

"Aren't we all?" asked Helen Wetherall with her plaintive, brave smile.

We stood under the chestnut trees for half an hour while the rain came down in sheets and the wind whistled and moaned and branches creaked like doors with stiff hinges. Linda and Valerie were both terribly wet for the wind had caught their plastic macs and blown them sideways. The rest of the trekkers had wet legs but fairly dry backs and shoulders.

At last a jagged patch of silver shone like a lighted window in the charcoal sky; the wind quietened and the rain lost its force. Michael brought out the map.

"Only four miles to our stopping place for the night," he said. "I hope the fairies have put the sticks in a dry spot. I volunteer here and now to get the fire going. I got my cub's badge for fire-lighting when I was eight."

"Bravo!" said Igor with, I thought, a touch of irony.

"And Sandy shall be my helper."

"Sandy must help with the horses," said Jonathan.

"I'll do one and then the other," I put in quickly.

Presently we continued our journey, with Linda firmly riding behind me. "I shall never manage four miles," she said. "I shall faint. I'm so tired."

But she looked a good colour and when I questioned her she could clearly remember her fall and the events preceding it so I decided that she was not concussed, particularly as there were no marks on her crash cap.

After a time Igor began to sing Russian songs. "To

keep up the spirits," he explained, and his baritone voice was so fine that not even Jonathan complained.

Presently, as the ground became lighter underfoot, we trotted, on and on until the steam rose from the ponies' backs and even Linda looked warmer. The rain gradually stopped and the sky cleared and now and then a brave bird broke into song.

"Down there," cried Michael suddenly. "Down there, where the lane winds, is our stopping place. Do you see a grey building, long and low, built against that outcrop of rock? Well, according to my map and Jake's written instructions, that's it. We'll soon get a blazing fire going to dry our clothes and warm us up."

"And brandy, we need brandy," said the Professor, wiping rain from his glasses. "Perhaps there is an inn nearby."

"Vodka it's more efficient, pure spirit, you see, like fire in your belly and sunshine on your heart!" cried Igor, waving his arms. "Oh, what would I give for a glass of vodka!"

"Aren't we getting romantic?" mocked Jonathan, not realising that the last remnants of wind would carry his voice forward. "It's all bogus, anyone can see *he* was never in the Revolution!"

Igor swung his pony round, his dark eyes blazing and his sturdy body somehow poised for action. He was almost inarticulate with passion. "I will never forgive you. Never! And you just a, a—a weak-kneed, hipped, how do you say it?—a weakling hippie who has done *nothing*, I tell you, *nothing*! You could not even manage the gentle Rolo, and you dare to call *me* a liar, a famous translator, a fighter in the cause of freedom. You are not a man. You are a boy who has not grown up, a sibling!"

Jonathan's pale eyes gazed in dismay, at the bearded

man before him, his mouth fell open. He shifted uneasily in his saddle. And now the following silence seemed potent with the Russian's anger. I shook myself.

"We are all hungry," I began, like a nanny with a bunch of naughty children, "and tired and edgy. Jonathan was only joking. Don't let's argue; let's get on and cook our supper, and then we'll all feel better."

"I apologise," said Jonathan, "unconditionally. I should not have insulted you. I don't know why I did. Sandy is right. Today has been a disaster. I over-reacted."

"Apology accepted absolutely," said the Russian with a generous wave of his hand. "Your accusation has flown away on the wind like a bad smell, and is forgiven."

We rode on again and soon we saw at last that a stone building was indeed beginning to take shape before our eyes, and never have I been gladder to see shelter, bringing with it the hope of food and warmth. The place turned out to be another deserted cottage.

"Is that *it*?" cried Valerie. "I tell you straight I'm not sleeping in *there*. It will be riddled with rats and mice."

"I thought we were all accustomed to vermin by now. They are part of the holiday adventure," said Eric Small with a nasty edge to his voice.

"Let's discuss that after we have eaten. We must deal with the inner man first," said the Professor.

"For 'adventure' read 'discomfort'," said Eric Small.

"Oh, Eric," lamented Mrs. Wetherall, "I thought you had more guts than that. 'Laugh and the world laughs with you, cry and you cry alone'."

"Now then, I vote that Kristianne and Fergie are in charge of the ponies," said Michael, throwing his reins to Felicity, "with the twins as assistants, and Sandy and I set to work getting supper under way. I hope the fairies have left us plenty of beer."

"Well said!" cried Jane. "Give me your noble steed, Sandy." I dismounted and found my legs stiff as stilts, through sitting in one position in partly wet clothes. Awkwardly I followed Michael into the deserted cottage which smelt of damp and chicken droppings.

"I don't think Jake has chosen well this time," I said.

"Nor have the fairies," called Michael, "there's nothing here, no stocks, no beer, no food, no nothing."

"There *must* be, there's got to . . ." As I spoke I felt immeasurably tired.

"Well, there ain't," said Michael, coming out, and I must say I had to admire his composure. "So what next?"

"Let's go down to the farm, perhaps provisions were left there. Or there might be a message awaiting us. Don't let's tell the others or someone may lose his temper."

"Right, quick march!"

As we walked down the hill, I thought of the little dark woman at the bed and breakfast place, who had not expected us because of Jake's accident. Wasn't it possible that the fairies had made the same mistake? Who were the fairies anyway? Jake's joke had now become a horrible inconvenience.

"Didn't he give you their names and addresses?" asked Michael, whose mind must have been on the same track.

"No," I said miserably. "For some reason he didn't even tell us their names at any time. Jake likes mysteries. It's the whimsical side of his nature."

The farm house seemed deserted and, although we banged on the back and front doors and shouted ourselves nearly hoarse, there was no sound within, not even a dog barked.

"It's because of Jake's accident," I explained at last. "Everyone supposes that the trek is at an end."

"Is there a pub around? Let's look at the map. It only

72

marks large hotels, but maybe there's a hamlet or something nearby."

There wasn't.

"But," said Michael, "this is an ordnance map and they mark telephone kiosks, so . . ."

"I could phone Dad—he will take things in hand. Or my mother—she's enormously efficient."

"There are all our wet clothes to dry. Mind you, we can light a fire, there's plenty of wood around. Look at all those broken bits of fence over there."

Suddenly I began to feel better.

"Yes, here we are," said Michael. "T for telephone, not so far away, up on that road over there."

He pointed. "Shall we walk or go back for a moment?" I looked over his shoulder. "It's only about half a mile, isn't it? Let's run."

We jogged down the lane to a wide black road running between firs and here we were in luck, for a farmer stopped and, leaning out from his Land Rover, called "Want a lift?"

He drove us up to the kiosk which stood at the crest of the hill. The drive only took about three or four minutes and then I was dialling home. There was no answer for ages and I was just about to give up in despair when Mummy's voice gave our number.

"You're puffing," I said. "I'm sorry."

"I was feeding the hens when I heard it ringing. Anything wrong, darling?"

I explained, and after a pause she said, "Listen, Sandy, your father's out now but as soon as he's back he'll come and fetch you all in the mini-bus, and I'll have a meal waiting. All right?"

"Oh great," I said. "Mum, you're marvellous."

"Address," she said. "Where are you? Where's the empty cottage? Your father has to find you."

"I'll hand you over to Michael," I replied. "He's our map reader and very efficient."

When we returned to the cottage everyone seemed to be milling around except Linda, who was sitting on an old box and saying over and over again: "This is my last adventure holiday, and wagons and horses won't drag me into that cottage."

I cleared my voice. "There's no food," I announced, "and no drink, because we've got a special treat for you all; a party, in a warm kitchen with a lovely aga stove and tables and chairs and glasses."

"You're joking and this is no joking matter," said Eric Small.

"Where's the nearest pub?" asked Jonathan.

"It's true, and we are now going to light a fire to warm everybody while we are waiting."

"There's no one at the farmhouse down there. I've been down and had a look," said Jonathan. "You can't have *me* on."

"A mini-bus is collecting us. My Dad is coming, so cheer up, Linda, civilisation is at hand." I felt rather important at breaking the news, and grateful to Michael who had suggested how it should be done.

"So you've rung home. Well done!" said Fergie. "Good old Mum and Dad! The poor ponies had no feeds but the grass is lush, and we've turned them out in an empty field with sound fencing."

There was dry straw in the cottage which we used instead of paper, and plenty of broken lathes from the rotting ceiling, so it wasn't long before a fire blazed and we all began to feel better.

Within an hour Dad arrived, and soon afterwards we

were speeding homewards in the white mini-bus to wash in gloriously hot water and brush our hair in front of a mirror. In our village the local shopkeepers will open up in emergencies and they had obliged Mummy with tins of stewed steak, so that she had been able to make a splendid Hungarian goulash followed by rhubarb crumble with cream or custard, and biscuits and cheese. There was beer or cider and eventually brandy or madeira for those who wanted it, while in the boiler room wet clothes dried. Dad said he would go up that night to see Jake's wife and find out who the fairies were.

"I'll see you have provisions tomorrow evening even if if I have to take them myself," he said. "And we'll put a bag of oats in the bus, so that the ponies have a decent breakfast."

"And, Linda, do stay the night here and sleep in a warm bed," suggested Mummy, "if you feel you can't spend another night roughing it."

"May I think about it? I don't want to admit defeat," said Linda.

Igor told us funny stories and Professor Gray spoke of his time as a secret service man in wartime Italy and suddenly we seemed like a team, all agreeing, all laughing together.

Mummy had taken a lot of bread out of the deep freeze and a great piece of ham which she put into a large bag with a pound of butter and three knives.

"Now you can make yourselves sandwiches before you start tomorrow, and here are some tomatoes too, and you'll have to survive on biscuits for pudding because that's all I can spare. And here are fourteen eggs for breakfast and an old frying pan."

The Russian gave a bow. "Mrs. Hamilton, you are a real lady," he said, and Professor Gray kissed her hand.

"Now I'll run you back," said Dad. "Linda, which is it to be?"

"The mice," she said. "I'll risk them just once more."

"Brave girl," said Eric Small. "It's easy for Sandy, she's been brought up with livestock, but you have had to conquer a real and terrible fear, and that needs courage."

And so we went back to the cottage, full and warm, and slept soundly on the straw in our sleeping bags and for once I didn't wake first but dreamed on till eight o'clock.

CHAPTER SIX

FRIDAY

"Dad took me aside yesterday to say we must try to find the torc," said Fergie, as we walked back from the farmhouse where we had managed to obtain a jar of instant coffee, two pints of milk, a pound of sugar, and a kettle of boiling water.

"What does he expect us to do?"

"Carry out a search."

"Not really? I don't want to pry among other people's belongings."

"He says Jake is upset about losing it. Dad's been back again to look by the cottage and he also walked right down to the farm where they took Jake on the hurdle. Jake is convinced that one of the trekkers picked up the torc. He suspects Jonathan."

"Oh, no! He may be weak, but he's not a thief!" Now I had grown to like the trekkers and didn't want to admit that one of them might steal from an injured man.

"Well, will you search the girls' saddle bags, while I look at the boys?"

"Girls and boys! You can't call the Professor a boy!"

"Oh, don't be difficult, Sandy!" cried Fergie, his lean face full of consternation. "I don't want to do it either. But we owe it to Jake. He's been a good friend, hasn't he?"

"All right, I'll try. But if I'm caught I shall never live down my feelings of shame."

"Don't be priggish. Pretend you are a policewoman or a secret agent or something, if that helps," suggested Fergie. "And choose your moment carefully. I'll try to get all the girls—sorry, women I mean females—to come and catch the ponies with me."

"Kristianne tries to keep them away from you," I said.

"Don't be ridiculous," retorted Fergie, turning a little red.

The trekkers saw us coming and a cheer went up as they noted the jar of coffee and the steaming kettle.

Michael had lit a fire and Mummy's frying pan was heating up on top. We popped the fried eggs straight on to buttered bread and they tasted delicious, as almost everything does if you eat out in the fresh air with a breeze coming down from the hills.

After we had eaten, Fergie said, "Now let's tack up," and gave me a meaning look.

The trekkers fetched their saddles and bridles from the cottage.

"We can leave our saddle bags, because we shall be coming down here, so there's no point in lugging them over to the field," said Fergie.

"How do you know you put the ponies in the right field?" I asked.

"We don't, but I went right round and I know there were no gaps in the fencing and no open gates, and, although the grass was lush, it definitely wasn't shut up for hay."

We started walking down a track with Fergie leading the way, each carrying a dandy brush, hoof pick, head-collar and our pony's tack.

When we got to the field I said I had forgotten something. I carefully put my saddle on the fence, hung up my bridle and went back. Inside the cottage the light was dim and the air musty. I went into the room used by the females of the party and started going through the saddle bags with my heart beating quickly. Pyjamas, handkerchiefs, sponges, soap, make-up, hand cream, socks, pencils, money, paperback books—someone had even brought a tin of talcum powder as though she had hoped for a bath or a civilised wash every so often.

"Sandy?"

A figure darkened the doorway. It was Michael.

"What are you doing?"

"Looking for the torc, of course." I tried to sound matter-of-fact as I looked into the boy's rather square face.

"Secret service agent Sandy," he said with a grin. "Who will search mine—Fergie? I suppose I *am* a suspect, otherwise you would have let me into the secret."

"Everyone *must* be, no favouritism," I said, trying to sound cool.

"Found anything?"

"As a matter of fact I haven't."

"Well, I've come back for that sack of oats. It seems as though the ponies must feed off the ground today. Mind you, they are all blown out with grass and not the least bit hungry. But Fergie said the effects of the grass would wear off within a couple of hours, and then the oats would liven them up."

I felt quickly in the last saddle bag, not wanting to bring out the contents in front of Michael.

"Finished," I said. "Now I'll help you with the oats."

"I don't need help, thanks—not with the lifting, I mean, but I should welcome your company."

I looked at Michael and wished that he would let his hair grow.

"Why don't you?" I began.

"Why don't I what?"

"Let your hair grow."

"Like a pop star?"

"No, just a bit. Why, even Dad has longer hair than you. A little more would do so much for your profile."

"Thanks," said Michael.

"What for?"

"The advice."

"Oh, you're welcome," I said.

The ride went well that day and smoothly, too, because all the ponies were now accustomed to their riders and the general routine. We found a village and bought ourselves sandwiches at a pub, and the adults drank spirits or wine and the rest of us shandy or cider. Fergie kept shooting meaning glances in my direction and I knew he wanted me to take the males off somewhere so that he could look in their saddle bags. At last I confided in Michael.

"We must leave Fergie behind," I told him, "and remove everyone else."

"Yes. I take your point."

He looked at the map.

"There's an interesting church and a little river at the bottom of the hill. Shall we walk down and have a look?" he asked in a loud voice.

The Professor drained the last of his brandy.

"Ah, wonderful," he said.

"I feel like splashing cool water on my face," said Felicity. "Let's run down the hill, shall we, Jane?"

"Is the church mediæval?" asked Jonathan.

"I don't know, the map doesn't say."

"I'm willing," said Helen Wetherall. "But who will watch our noble steeds?"

"I will," offered Fergie. "I'm not the least interested in churches."

"Is there a shop down there?" asked Linda.

"Bound to be," I said.

"A Post Office? I must write to my mother. I need stamps."

One by one the trekkers were lured down the hill.

"I'll help you, Fergie," offered Michael. "Sandy had to let me into the secret, because I caught her searching bags in the cottage."

The ponies were tied to a fence, their saddles in a line nearer the pub, still with bags attached. Fergie and Michael started at different ends.

"I'll go down and try to keep the rest of the trekkers out of the way," I said.

When I returned I knew by Fergie's face that he had not discovered the torc among any of the male trekkers' belongings, and afterwards I started to eye the pockets in everyone's coats, looking vainly for tell-tale bulges; the only suspicious bulge was caused by the Professor's jack-knife.

Riding on, Fergie and Kristianne led the way, talking and laughing and forgetting about everyone else. The sun came out, and in the fields the lambs danced and played. It was hard to think of thieves and treachery.

"I'm glad I stuck it out," said Linda. "It was the wet that got me down."

She patted her pony's neck. "I shall miss you, Toffee, when I get home," she added.

We lost our way in the afternoon. Fergie blamed Michael for poor map reading, but I think Jake's instructions were muddling, and it was late when at last we found the farm where we were to spend the night. This time our sleeping place was to be a great stone and timber barn, by a cold water tap, in which a sack of oats and boxes of provisions awaited us.

Now the fairies seemed to have excelled themselves, as though to make up for their mistake the previous day. A beautiful fireplace had been built under a shelter with a corrugated iron roof. A grid had been put ready, with twenty-eight pieces of chicken, a great bag of brown and white rolls, three bags of tomatoes, one of courgettes and four enormous tins of oxtail soup plus a large saucepan in which to cook it. For pudding there was a basket of fruit —grapes, oranges, apples and bananas—and a Wensleydale cheese together with two packets of crackers and three blocks of butter. For breakfast we found a jar of honey, four loaves, a dozen eggs and a bag of sliced bacon. A note told us to go to the farm for milk, tea and coffee. Opening a cardboard box, we uncovered twenty cans of beer, and three bottles of lemon barley water.

"Your father has used his influence," said Valerie. "He looks an influential sort of person. A boss."

"Oh, I wouldn't say that. He's an individual," suggested Fergie.

"A charming man, handsome, and very Scottish, if I may be personal," put in Kristianne.

"They've forgotten the hurricane lamps, and I haven't any matches. Jonathan, a match?" asked Michael, who was itching to light the fire.

"Run out."

"I'll go to the farm," offered Igor.

"I'll come too," I said.

Dusk was falling like a curtain over the landscape, obliterating the hills one by one and everything was very still without bird-song or wind, or even, it seemed, the buzz and movement of insects.

We went round to the back of the shabby white farm-house, and, stepping over innumerable empty tin dishes, reached the chipped back door. A dozen or so thin cats watched us with wide hungry eyes. We pressed a bell and waited, and then the door opened cautiously to reveal a plump woman with curly hair, bulging peat-dark eyes and a pinky-brown face.

"A match, I wonder . . ." began Igor, his beard and moustache parting to show excellent front teeth.

A look of intense fear crossed the woman's face.

"Not you!" she cried and slammed the door.

We heard bolts being pushed into place, a chain fixed, and then two disappointed little brown and white cats started to mew pathetically.

"Why me? What is wrong with me? Sandy, I ask you, I ask you plainly, do I have the face of a devil or what?" Igor threw up his arms, his mouth twisted in perplexity. "What have I done to deserve such treatment?"

"Have you never seen her before? Does she mean nothing to you?" My voice sounded dramatic, for to tell the truth I was shaken. Who was Igor Polunsky? Where did he come from? A famous translator, he had said, and a campaigner for freedom? Now all sorts of wildly improbable pictures flashed before my eyes. Secret agent? Communist spy? K.G.B.?

"Meanwhile, we have no match, and Michael is champing at our headquarters because he cannot light the fire, and we need coffee and milk."

"Yes!" I said.

"I promise you, Sandy, I cross my heart, I swear, that I am no devil, no mystery man, just a Russian refugee earning an honest living in London and meeting with other refugees to discuss how to help those who fight for freedom, for natural human rights in Soviet Russia. My conscience is as clear as a mountain stream."

"Yes, of course I believe you, Igor."

It was true; looking at his kindly countenance, the brown eyes and the smile that crinkled his face, I felt happy again in his company. Those fleeting feelings of suspicion were no more than a bad dream, a disgraceful moment of distrust.

"Look," I said. "We are only a few miles from home. I know this area a little bit, and there's a pub only a few hundred yards away. Let's go there for matches."

"Right, at your command," said Igor. "Come on," he laughed. "The devil will take you. I shall never forget that woman's face," he continued. "The sheer terror. I might have been her executioner, poor thing! Do you think she is locking the doors at this very moment? It is strange, isn't it? Am I another man's double? It is like one of your ridiculous, corny—corny, is the right word?—television programmes."

"Perhaps she is mad," I said. "Perhaps every bearded man reminds her of some nightmare. Perhaps she forgot to take her tranquillisers."

"Oh, Sandy, you English children are so wise for your years, it troubles me. You know so much."

"Just now I feel a hundred. Look, there are the lights of the pub," I said. It was a white, slate-roofed building on the corner of the road, with roses climbing on the walls and honeysuckle sweetly scenting the night air.

"Good. You know, I must tell you, Sandy, that I think I have been the luckiest rider. My horse—I refuse to call him a pony, for he is every inch a horse—my Cadbury is such a staunch fellow, so kind and always willing. He has never given me one moment's anxiety and that makes me very happy. You understand?"

"Yes."

"He is like a kind nurse to me, a children's nanny. He puts his head down each morning so that I can easily slip the bridle over his ears, he fits his head into his head-collar when I go to catch him up, and he lifts, he actually lifts, each foot in turn for me to pick it out. I do not have to speak, to command. He does all these things without a word being spoken."

"That means he likes you," I said.

"You really think so?"

"I am certain."

"And Rolo did not like the student?"

"Absolutely."

We had reached the pub now.

"Do you have to stay outside? I want to buy wine, for this is the last night and we must celebrate."

"I can come in so long as I'm not served with an alcoholic drink, at least I think so," I said.

We went into the public bar which was crowded. As Igor elbowed his way through the drinkers a silence fell, and I supposed that we looked a strange pair, a dark, rather wild-looking man with a bushy beard and eyes so nearly black that they could not belong to anyone of British blood, and a fair girl. Indeed, I knew that Igor's darkness only accentuated my fairness.

"Ah, wine, have you two bottles of good French wine? Claret, I think—no, three bottles, please. And a box of matches—no, three boxes of matches."

The man behind the bar looked Igor up and down as though he was a strange being from outer space.

"Just a minute," he said after a pause. "I'll have a look. Hold on, will you?"

"Hold on? Hold on to what?"

"He means *wait a minute*."

I was horribly aware that a small knot of men had gathered round us. Tough muscular men, with brown faces and arms accustomed to turning the steering wheels of huge tractors or lifting hay or handling unpredictable bulls.

"Michael will be mad by now, with the fire laid and the night coming and no light to send a flame into life," said Igor.

"I hope they won't be worried at our disappearance."

"They will know you are quite safe with me."

"Come far?" a burly farmer asked in a broad Shropshire accent.

"London," replied Igor.

"He means today," I said, and then added to the man, "No, from the farm down the road. We are pony trekking."

"Oh, ah!"

"And we have no match to light a fire," said Igor. "Listen, if the wine will take a long time to find, let us just have the matches."

"What are you going to burn?"

"Chicken, we cook chicken, and eat it in our hands, so. We are like savages. I have not changed my clothes for a week. I have lived like a soldier at the front. Each morning I wash in cold water, and Sandy, too."

"A likely story," said a blonde woman, sipping a glass of sweet sherry. "Like savages, eh? How romantic."

"You do not believe me? You think I make it up?" Igor swung round. "Madam, I ask you to remember that

86

I may be a foreigner but I am also a gentleman. I come here to buy wine, not to be insulted."

The publican now returned. "How's this?" He offered Igor a bottle of pale wine the colour of raspberry-flavoured penicillin.

"That is rosé. I asked for claret. Never mind, just the matches, please? I do not like this place. There is no hospitality. In my country . . ."

" 'Ang on a minute."

"Don't say you have no matches. What is wrong with Shropshire? I do not understand. You do not have to search for *matches*!" ·

"Let's go," I urged, feeling a new surge of hostility around us. "There's something odd going on." Perhaps, I thought, everyone but I can see a strange madness in his face, an evilness that terrifies. "Come on, Igor," I added. "They don't mean to get the matches. Let's go." I was suddenly aware that I had become bossy during the last few days, and accustomed to telling grown-ups what to do. I was only a child, yet taking charge.

But we couldn't get through. The crowd of men hemmed us in.

"What's the hurry?" asked a small ferret-faced man, his arms bulging with muscle. "Scared?"

"Here, I've laid my hands on three bottles of claret, vintage stuff. Come on, have a look. I've been down the cellar for you."

"Yes, and that's a risk—there are vampires in *his* cellar," called a jovial red-faced man with a stomach as round as a barrel.

"This place stifles me!" cried Igor. "I need the fresh air."

"And what are you doing with a little girl? *She's* not

your daughter!" said the blonde woman, putting down her sherry glass. "Are you going to cook her along with the chicken?"

"Don't be ridiculous. I'm leading the trek," I shouted.

"I bet you are," cried a youth.

"Come over here, dear, I want to talk to you," said the blonde woman. "Come on," she beckoned with a ringed finger. Her eyes were very blue, like the jet of a gas fire before it changes to gold, and she spoke kindly.

"I've got to see to the ponies," I said.

Igor started to use his elbows, but to no avail. However much we pushed we seemed to remain in the centre of a circle of suspicious men.

Now the Russian started to clench his fists and I thought: he's going to try to fight his way out, and, although he may be as strong as a bear, he can't take on all of them.

"Why are you keeping us? Let me give you my parents' address if you don't believe I'm one of the leaders of a trek. Then you can phone them and satisfy yourselves," I said, and my voice seemed detached from me, someone else's voice playing a part that was not made for me, for I was growing frightened and a nagging hunger began to produce a sensation of disembodiment which was very strange.

"They think I am a big bad man who has kidnapped you, a poor helpless little girl," said Igor hoarsely. "That is the only explanation. I am guilty of nothing."

"You have no right to keep us here," I said. "Please move." Then the door opened and two policemen came in.

"Where is he?"

"Here."

They grabbed Igor before he had time to do more than let out an exclamation in Russian which no one understood.

"I'm sorry, sir, you will have to come along to the station with us, and you too, miss."

"Well, so long as we can clear up this matter," said Igor more calmly. "I am a Russian emigrant on an adventure holiday."

"We'll take the statement at the station and we shall need your fingerprints, sir."

"But why?" I asked.

"They've been living like savages, *together*," said the blonde. "He hasn't changed his clothes for days."

The policemen frisked Igor to make sure he was not armed. Then as they walked him across the room one either side, the door opened and in walked Professor and Mrs. Gray.

"Oh, there you are! We were getting a little worried," said the Professor, goggling a little behind his glasses as his eyes tried to adjust to the brightness after the dark outside. "We've got coffee and milk from the farm and Michael has lit the fire and the chicken is cooking nicely. We came up here to buy a few bottles of wine as we think the last night calls for a little celebration."

"Geoffrey! Can't you see there's trouble, the police, Geoffrey," hissed Mrs. Gray.

The Russian cleared his throat as though about to make a speech.

"It appears that I am under arrest. England is not a free country after all. An honest citizen cannot buy a bottle of wine without risking arrest and interrogation. It may interest you to know, Professor, that I am now on my way to the police station. It appears that friendly Russians are not to be tolerated in these parts." Igor's voice was scornful, his lip curled like an angry Kerry Blue dog's. "What is it the youngsters call them—fizz, isn't it—the fizz, as you

89

see here, have, in their wisdom, decided to deprive me of my freedom."

I thought that Igor was overreacting, for the police had been remarkably gentle and polite.

Mrs. Gray planted herself in the doorway. "Why are you arresting our Russian friend?" she demanded.

"Only taking him away for questioning, madam, after a phone call," said the taller of the two policemen.

"He has made a naughty phone call? Oh, Igor, surely not!" cried Mrs. Gray.

"No, madam. It could be a more serious charge."

"Do none of you crazy trekkers read the newspapers?" asked the blonde woman. "Are you not aware that a dangerous man with a black beard and foreign accent is on the run after assaulting women?"

The Professor burst into a shout of laughter. "Igor dangerous? Assaulting women? He's the gentlest person I've ever known! Oh, my dear fellows, you are certainly barking up the wrong tree. Besides, he has an alibi. When did the last assault take place?"

"Yesterday evening between ten and eleven o'clock, sir," said the younger of the two policemen, loosening his grip on Igor's arm.

"Well then, he was with us and Sandy's parents. We were all having a jolly meal together down at the farm."

"And where's that?"

I told the police my parents' names and address.

"So you would be Miss Hamilton, then?"

They fetched out their notebooks and eventually, after further questioning, they let Igor go and drove off to see my parents. The publican started to apologise, but Igor left the pub without a word. Following with Mrs. Gray, I saw that his hands were shaking.

"I need a cigarette but I do not smoke now," he said pathetically.

"A wretched experience, but all's well that ends well," put in Mrs. Gray in a bracing voice, touching his arm as she spoke.

"Do I look like that, do I look as though I assault women?"

"No, of course not. You look like a great Hebrew prophet, only nicer," replied Mrs. Gray.

Later that evening, cheered by a good meal, three glasses of the Professor's claret and a blazing fire, Igor felt better. His eyes were warm again in his friendly face, his cheeks glowed, and waving one hand he said. "Do you remember how in *War and Peace* when the Count is dying, the great scenes of his life pass before his eyes? Well, when I die, this marvellous moment will pass before *my* eyes, the blazing fire, the horses looking at us over the hedge, the ancient barn that has seen so much, your faces, the old and the young, this will be the vision, the memory that will brighten the last hours of my life."

"My dear Igor! How charming, how touching," cried the Professor. "Let us drink to Igor. Come on, be up-standing for a toast to our great Russian patriot and friend, Igor Polunsky."

We stood and drank his health in plastic cups, and then Mrs. Grey cleared her throat and, pushing a strand of grey hair back in the direction of her bun, she said:

"Well now, we have all been merry and happy, but there is one serious matter that cannot be ignored—I mean, of course, the fact that a dangerous man is on the run around here. Someone must guard the young girls in our party."

"I volunteer to take one watch," said Michael promptly.

"Me too," said Fergie.

"You are so young, Fergie," said Helen Wetherall. "We really need a man to deal with a maniac."

"I think there should be a watch of two," suggested Jonathan, "I would not want to tackle him alone."

"He will be most frightened by me," said Igor with a grin, "for I am his double and what could be more terrifying than coming face to face with yourself! He will think he's drunk or mad or even dead and about to meet his God!"

"I shan't sleep a wink," said Valerie. "I'm glad it's the last night, I really am. There have been too many scares."

"Now, you ladies get ready for bed and we men will promise to guard you most carefully," said the Professor in a fatherly voice. "Sandy, you are quite dark under the eyes, off you go now!"

I didn't like being treated like a child again, but I went just the same, and as I walked to the barn I heard Eric Small say in his rather prissy voice, "Well, we asked for adventure and we've certainly got it." And the Professor said, "One more glass of wine to warm the cockles of the heart, yes?"

"I feel quite sad, I really do," remarked Linda as we undressed. "And to think that this time tomorrow I shall be in my own warm little bed in Croydon, with a duvet, if you please, ever so cosy against my chin."

"Those men!" I said. "Talk about sex equality! There they are, sending us off to bed as though we are a lot of Victorians to be ordered about by their menfolk, while *they* stay on drinking by the camp fire."

"I think it is so nice that they are protective," retorted Helen Wetherall. "The age of chivalry is not yet dead, my dear."

We were to sleep in straw in a section of the barn fenced off by a rough timber partition. When we had washed under the tap, cleaned our teeth and slipped into our sleeping bags, a couple of thin cats came to join us, having feasted on the remains of our grilled chicken.

I was tired; my eyelids felt as though they were weighted with lead and the darkness wrapped me round like a blanket. Within moments I must have been asleep.

CHAPTER SEVEN

SATURDAY

I dreamed that the torc had been stolen by my father. Returning home I found it glistening round my mother's neck. "Look, Sandy," she said, "look at this wee pre-Roman necklace! Doesn't it suit me? And Jake will never know, for Jake has gone."

"Gone where?"

But now another voice answered. "Wake," it said. "Wake up! There's a shadow across the barn. Sandy! The man! Call the Professor."

Felicity was looking down at me, her blue eyes dizzy with fear, her fair hair all fluffy round her bright startled face.

"The guard," I said, trying to pull myself out of the dream into reality. "The torc, no, I mean the guard—where is the guard?"

I sat up. The night was more grey than black, and there *was* a shadow across the doorway, but not the shape of a man.

"It's not two-legged, or human," I hissed.

And then the shadow came in, took solid form and I saw that it was Mimosa.

"Oh, you wicked pony!"

She came across, looking very sweet, her hooves quiet on the straw-strewn floor, and nuzzled me.

"That means all the ponies are out," said Felicity. "We had better dress and investigate."

"And meet the maniac."

I slipped out of bed, dragged a coat and jodhpurs over my pyjamas and then put my arms round Mimosa's neck for a moment, feeling her warmth. Outside I found the Professor brandishing an incredibly sharp pointed stick.

"See," he said, "it's better than a bayonet. I made it with the help of my jack-knife. Why are you up? Girls are not guarding." He lunged at an imaginary object.

"Didn't you see the pony?"

"Yes, but she only went in to feed, didn't she? I mean, she's a gentle creature."

"But the others might be out?"

"No, they are watching us over the hedge. We are their telly programme. Look."

And indeed thirteen equine faces were watching us with alert dark eyes.

"We must find the hole in the fence," said Felicity, who had also dressed. "Come on."

"A guard," said the Professor. "Eric, Eric! Don't say the wretched man has fallen asleep while on duty? He could face court martial or worse for that."

The librarian sauntered round the corner. "Nothing to report," he said.

"Escort these girls, please. They have to investigate a gap in the hedge."

The birds were beginning to sing as the sun streaked the eastern sky with pink and gold. The dew silvered every blade and stem and flower; there was a lovely smell of wet grass, and the breath of ponies. Silverstar walked with us right round the field, nuzzling my pockets for oats or cubes. She looked very beautiful in the dawn, like something out of a fairy tale.

"Mimosa has always been a getter-out," I said. "If there is a gap she will find it and enlarge it."

"The Professor has more courage than sense," said Eric Small. "He thinks he could kill a man with that spear he's made."

"I think so, too," said Felicity.

We found the gap, and Silverstar nibbled my back affectionately as I lent down to try to pull two broken strands of wire across it. Her breath was very warm and her whiskers tickled the gap between my jodhpurs and sweater.

Then suddenly Eric froze.

"There's a man," he said in a horrified whisper. "Look, walking towards the barn. D'ye see the top of his head?"

"Has he got a thick black beard? It's probably Igor taking an early morning constitutional," I said.

"No," said Felicity. "He isn't. He's a stranger with black hair."

"Back to the farm, that's an order," said Eric.

I gave a last wrench at the wire and straightened my back. I didn't feel frightened. There had been too many false alarms.

"All right."

We walked back across the field, Eric striding ahead.

"Professor," he called, as we reached the barn, "prepare to make an arrest. There's a man with dark hair coming this way."

"They frisked Igor, which suggests the villain is armed," I said, beginning to feel a tingle of excitement. "But we don't want anyone killed."

"I take your point," Eric said. "I will engage him in conversation, Professor, while you hide in the barn with your spear and watch."

"No, I am better at talking," argued the Professor, "and I am older than you. My career is almost over, so if someone is to be shot it had best be me, and please call me

Geoffrey—everyone else does. Here, take my spear! He is almost with us. Quick, get ready! Sandy, in the barn please!"

The man who now approached was indeed dark, but small and not bearded. Instead his chin was rough with stubble. But then, I thought, he could have shaved after the last assault.

"Good morning," called the Professor, in the most friendly of voices. "A lovely day, isn't it?"

"And who would you be?" asked the man.

"A trekker, one of Jake's trekkers, and who are you?"

"That's not your business now, is it?" The man gave a slow grin, then started to walk towards the barn.

"You can't go in there, there are ladies in there."

"Oh, ah," said the man, looking at the Professor rather oddly. "You've got ladies in there, 'ave you?"

"I think I had better go into action. It's getting nasty," said Eric, stepping out with the Professor's spear in his hand.

"And a friend, too, I see," added the man with a touch of mockery. "What might you be doing on Mr. Jones's farm?"

"That's what we are asking *you*," said Eric, brandishing the spear. "We are looking . . ."

"Sssh," hissed the Professor. "Let me handle this."

"And what might all these ponies be doing on Mr. Jones's farm?" continued the man, eyeing Eric with scorn. "Play acting, are you?"

Then Valerie stepped out of the barn wearing only pyjamas, gave a piercing scream and dashed back.

"He's there, he's there, the maniac! And Eric has a spear. He's threatening him."

At that moment, Mimosa, with extraordinary composure, walked across the yard and started to nuzzle the

D

dark man's pockets, and I said, "He must be all right. Ponies smell evil and back away."

The man pulled a lump of sugar out and fed it to her. "I work here," he said. "And I suppose you are Jake's adventure holiday—that was a mad notion if ever there was one. And damn me if he didn't go and break a leg, and now you are out and about on your own, knowing only half the business, with two kids in charge."

The Professor took off his bi-focal glasses, rubbed them with a blue handkerchief and returned them to his nose.

"I don't like your way of putting things," he said. "We have womenfolk here and a duty to protect them, especially when we have information that a dangerous man is on the loose."

"Caught him," said the man.

"What do you mean? What's that?"

"The police picked him up at midnight. He's under lock and key now. There was one false alarm from the lady down at the farm here, as it happens, but that turned out to be a Russian refugee."

"Me," said Igor, emerging from the barn with a broad smile on his face. "Good morning, Mimosa, so we are to have a pony for breakfast, are we?"

Now the man seemed taken aback. "I'm sorry I wasn't very civil, like," he said. "Mrs. Jones should have told me you would be here. Only seeing that Jake was laid up . . . I thought . . ."

"Please don't worry. Come and share our breakfast in half an hour's time, please do. We should be so delighted," said the Professor. "*We* hardly treated *you* in a civil manner."

"Thanks, but I must be seeing to the sheep," the man said and he strode away with the same spring in his gait that Jake has. Then I started to laugh. I don't know why, but the laugh seemed to catch hold of me and refuse to stop. I think it was the sight of Eric Small brandishing the home-made spear and the Professor goggling through his glasses that started me off inside, and now also the relief of knowing the man was just a farm worker and we were all safe, and this was the last day.

Fergie appeared as if from nowhere and said, "Sandy, Sandy! For heaven's sake, what's the joke?"

"The man," I tried to explain, "and these two were ready armed to the teeth and he was just a nice Shropshire shepherd." I began to laugh again. "Mimosa knew better," I gasped between great waves of laughter which seemed to threaten to engulf me.

"Oh, Fergie! What has happened? Why does your sister suffer from hysterics? She is like a little girl," said Kristianne, appearing in a glorious pair of pyjamas, which were chic enough to serve as a summer trouser suit. "And why is Mimosa here, standing about like another human being?"

"It's all a bit of mystery," said Fergie uneasily. "I suppose we ought to get a fire going."

"I'll help you," offered Kristianne, slipping her hand into my brother's.

My laughing stopped. I suddenly felt very young and stupid. Here was I, Sandy, one of the leaders of the trek, convulsed in idiotic laughter.

"Our last day," crooned Kristianne, gazing into Fergie's eyes—and for an awful moment I hated the Swedish girl. I wanted to scoop up mud in my hands to throw it at her gorgeous face, spoiling her lovely complexion and spattering her cheeks with dirt. I could not understand why.

The next minute Mimosa came walking out of the barn

99

carrying a loaf of bread in her mouth, her expression full of triumph, like a dog who has found a juicy bone.

"Fergie, catch her!" I shouted.

But our naughty palomino pony dodged my brother and with a glance at all her friends watching excitedly over the hedge, trotted off down the lane.

"I'll run after her," cried Felicity. "I'm very fast."

"No, she'll only go faster if she's chased. The bread won't be any good to us now, so we might as well leave her to eat it. She's sure to come back soon, because she hates being alone," said Fergie, disengaging his hand from Kristianne's affectionate grasp.

"Did the man come?" asked Helen Wetherall, emerging from the barn, rubbing her eyes.

"No, no. He's caught and under lock and key. You can all breathe again. Where's Michael? We need a fire and tea," said the Professor.

"Oh, darling Rolo, are you waiting for your auntie? Look, isn't he sweet? Rolo, I've saved you a lump of sugar. Just a minute, pet."

Mrs. Wetherall picked her way round the mud, her feet in pale blue bedroom slippers which looked a little odd with riding kit. "There are you, ducky—is it good?"

Fergie started to pick up a few sticks, while I stirred the ashes in the fireplace. They were still hot and glimmers of red shone in the grey. Felicity filled a pan of water from the top.

"Not too full," advised the Professor. "Just enough for the three or four of us here, and then put on more for the rest who are not up yet. After all, it's only half past six."

Mimosa came back and stood by the fire resting a leg, a look of benign contentment on her wide face.

"She's like a big dog," said Helen Wetherall.

"She's feeling superior because all the others are on the wrong side of the fence. She knows they are envious. Look at their expressions," I said. And it was true. The other ponies were watching Mimosa avidly and every now and then Silverstar leaned against the hedge, as though hoping it would give way so allowing her to join her friend.

"Sometimes she slips into the kitchen at home and stands by the Aga stove," said Fergie. "One day she brought her foal, Noodles, along with her."

"Unbelievable," enthused Kristianne.

Three hours later, we were winding our way homewards.

"The last day," sighed Jane. "And it's been such fun."

"Will you do it again next year, Sandy?" asked Michael.

"It's not for me to say," I answered, and at that very moment I only wanted to be back at our little farm, stretched out under a tree, reading a book. I was tired of responsibility. I wanted to look up from reading to see the sky through a tracery of leaves, and know that I could stay there another hour, away from school and people and decisions.

"I think I'm tired," I went on. "It must be because I feel depressed."

"That's because it's the last day," said Jane. "You know all the fun will be over soon and everyone will be catching trains or buses or driving cars right out of your life."

"No, it's not quite like that."

I was riding Silverstar, who was excited because she knew she was nearing home and every so often she saw a familiar landmark. She strode very fast, ahead of all the others and from time to time she jogged a few steps before I could bring her back to a walk.

Fergie was at the back with Kristianne inevitably beside

101

him, but Caramelo shared Silverstar's feelings and it was all the Swedish girl could do to keep her under control.

The skies were clear and May's sun was golden and warm on our backs, with its heat tempered by a little breeze from the south west. It was a perfect day for riding, with the broom on the hills bursting into bloom and wild flowers sparkling like thrown jewels in the glass. Helen Wetherall started to sing little ditties that bored Jonathan and brought tears of suppressed giggles to Felicity's eyes.

I wondered whether Jake was out of hospital and if he would be at his farm to greet us on our return, and whether he was still upset about the loss of the torc. I wondered also about a project I had completed at school just before half term on careers. Had I dealt too much with the professions and not enough with trades like plumbing and carpentry?

Then Linda's voice interrupted my thoughts:

"Sandy, Fudge is limping!"

I brought a reluctant Silverstar to a standstill, dismounted and led her back to where Linda was not holding the little liver chestnut mare, who looked at me very sweetly from under her forelock. Her wide blaze and big gentle eyes were endearing, and I patted her for a moment before picking up her near foreleg.

"I had just changed over with Valerie, who had been riding her till a few minutes ago," said Linda. "Then we decided to swop."

"There's nothing to see," I said, "but her actual hoof seems to feel a little warm. Fergie, what do you think?"

"She was all right with me," said Valerie.

"The fetlock and tendon are both cool—walk her forward, please," said Fergie, leaving Kristianne to hold Mimosa, who took the opportunity to bury her head in deep grass.

102

"Yes, she's lame all right. We've got about five miles to go."

"We mustn't ride a lame pony," I said.

"I expect I could manage five miles on my feet," said Linda. "So not to worry."

"No, we'll take it in turns," said Fergie. "You have Mimosa and I'll lead Fudge and then we'll swop. I reckon she has a bruised sole."

"I don't mind walking a mile or two," said Helen Wetherall. "In my youth I was a bit of a mountaineer."

"I think the young ones can manage this," said the Professor. "Us oldsters need to conserve our energy for the long journey home tonight."

Fergie walked about a mile and a half and then he rode Silverstar and I led Fudge, who put her chin on my shoulder and breathed against my cheek. Michael offered to take a turn but the Professor said we needed him as our map reader, and then Jonathan replaced me.

"No sight of the torc, someone *must* have nicked it," he whispered as he took Fudge's reins. Linda seemed to be happy with Mimosa, so I mounted Bullfinch, who was wide and rather wooden when it came to twisting or turning.

"Some people think it's you," I hissed, leaning down from my saddle.

"Me—what?"

"You, who took the torc." I smiled. "Ridiculous, isn't it?"

"You may not like me," he said angrily, "but I'm not the sort of person who would rob a wounded man!"

"No, but they have to suspect someone. Who do *you* think took it?"

"Helen Wetherall, she's the one person with the know-how."

"What do you mean?"

"Well, she's worked in a museum, hasn't she?"

"She's the *soul* of honour. Oh, Jonathan, you're way out." I couldn't resist laughing as I spoke, for it seemed ridiculous to suggest that the widow would steal.

"She needs the money. She told me that her husband left very little and her heating bills and income tax seem to take all she earns."

"Yes, but I'm sure she would rather die than steal."

We rode on. The sun grew hotter on our backs and the sky was as blue as a tranquil summer sea. All around us the animals of the wild, the rabbits, the birds, the voles, and so many others that we did not see but occasionally heard, continued living their own lives. We came to the top of a hill and looked down on a valley spread out before us like a tablecloth dotted with toys, tiny hedges, little houses and farm buildings. There was a church with an ancient tower and a clock, its hands obliterated for us by distance, bullocks and sheep, and miniature cars winding like dinky toys down curling ribbons of grey nylon. Here the breeze touched our faces and brought with it all the summer smells free from the blight of petrol fumes, the stink of factories or pollution.

"I feel like a king again," cried Igor. "Down there is my kingdom. I am King Offa! Do you not feel the presence of the great King Offa? I read a book about him before I came. Oh, this air is like wine! It intoxicates! Would you not agree, Professor?"

"Do call me Geoffrey, everyone else does. I want to forget my academic duties for one more day. Yes, Igor, it has a certain invigorating quality, I grant you that."

"But we are not yet on Offa's Dyke, are we, Michael?" said Eric Small.

"Well, don't let us be pedantic," cried Igor. "He saw

this place, he breathed the same air, felt the wind in his face . . ."

Behind me I could hear Kristianne's voice.

"You will write, Fergie, won't you? I'll give you my address. We must keep in touch."

At last, as a church clock struck twelve, we saw Jake's place perched halfway up a hill, an untidy sprawl of buildings, a lorry, a caravan and a couple of cattle trucks.

Now Caramelo and Silverstar danced and pranced the more, snorting and pulling and throwing their lovely heads in the air, while Bullfinch plodded dutifully with pricked ears and careful steps.

"I hope Jake's got a bumper plate of nosh for us. I'm starving," said Michael, putting the map away in his pocket.

"His place looks deserted," I said. "Look, can you see a single two-legged person? Those tiny dots are chickens, and there's a dog."

"Isn't there a restaurant in the village?"

"No, but the pub does snacks."

I was hungry, too. My stomach rumbled and at the very thought of food saliva rose to my mouth. I hoped desperately that Jake or the fairies had not let us down. If they had, Fergie and I would simply go home, but I wanted the trekkers to leave happily with full stomachs and literally with nice tastes in their mouths.

"There's no smoke. It's not going to be a camp fire meal this time."

"Probably supermarket fare, you know, cold meat pies and packet treacle tart," said Helen Wetherall. "I could eat *anything*."

"A long cool glass of beer—German lager, that's my choice," said the Professor.

"A white wine, cool as a mountain stream, straight from the refrigerator," suggested the Russian.

"You sound like an advertisement," said Jonathan. "Who's going to lead Fudge now . . . Kristianne?"

"Yes, certainly, but no one else can manage Caramelo," said the Swedish girl, "so I think I had better stay where I am, or would you like to try?"

Jonathan shook his head. "I'm yellow," he said.

"I'll take a turn," offered Jane. "Come on."

"But Peppermint can't take me, my feet would touch the ground," objected Jonathan.

"You have Bullfinch, I'll ride Peppermint. Are you sure you want to, Jane?" I slid to the ground. "It's only another mile at the very most."

"I'm not being churlish. It's simply that I want to arrive back *in* the saddle. It's a matter of prestige or something," confessed Jonathan.

Now the track wound downwards and there were gates to be opened and shut, and sheep gazed at us with bland almond eyes. I began to wonder what sort of welcome Learie, our collie, would give us and whether Mummy would have made a lovely goo-ey lardy cake for tea. And I saw myself sitting at our large kitchen table telling our parents our adventures, trying to describe without laughing the making of the spear and the moment when it was brandished so wildly at an innocent man by harmless-looking Eric.

Then suddenly there was a commotion behind us, a voice shouting a command in Swedish, and then the next moment Caramelo, who wanted to gallop the last stretch home, overtook little Peppermint and set off down the hill plunging and bucking. Kristianne sat as though glued to the saddle, her back stiff, her head high and her hands low either side of the mare's neck, level with the withers.

"I'm glad I'm yellow," said Jonathan in a flat voice. "That isn't quite my scene."

"Move, move out of the way," called Fergie, cantering after Kristianne.

"She'll only go faster if you chase her," I shouted.

"I'm not *chasing*, just going to pick up the pieces," said my brother, looking very stern.

"It's time she came off," said Jonathan. "She was too pleased with herself by half."

"Oh, don't be beastly," I retorted. "Supposing she's hurt. I don't even know where her people live."

"Fergie will."

"Oh, look," called Linda. "Her saddle bag's undone and things are falling out. Here's her comb and make-up things. Poor Kris! She must have filled it too full and the strain has bust the strap."

"And, oh dear, I mean, oh good, but here's something once important wrapped in her panties—Jake's torc!"

She held up the band of gold.

"The torc," cried Helen Wetherall. "Where, how ...?"

"You have found it!" exclaimed the Professor. "You clever girl." Then his voice also trailed away.

A silence followed while everyone tried to absorb the fact that Kristianne was the guilty member of the party.

"Well, I must say it's taken me by surprise," Michael at last. "I've suspected several people, but not Kristianne. Although my father always said 'never trust a foreigner'!"

"Well, that was very ignorant advice which I deplore," said the Professor sharply. "The English have no special premium on honesty."

"But such a beautiful girl," said his wife. "She looks as though butter wouldn't melt in her mouth."

"Don't you believe it," said Jonathan. "She's as cunning as a cat. And you all suspected me! I know, I felt your distrust."

"Now don't let's be unkind," cut in Helen Wetherall. "I am sure she took it in a moment of aberration and has been trying to confess ever since."

"I think she's eaten up by vanity. She simply wanted it," said Valerie. "Pretty girls are often like that They've been spoiled even as little children. They can get away with murder, while plain people have to work and struggle to get a few crumbs of appreciation." She spoke bitterly. Her jealousy was obvious.

Silence fell as Fergie and Kristianne came riding back.

"She's lost some things out of her saddle bag," called Fergie. "What are you all waiting for?"

"She had the torc," called Valerie. "She had the torc all the time hidden in her panties in the saddle bag. Look! Hold it up, Jane. Come on, don't be shy."

Jane held up the curved band of ornamented gold.

"And if Caramelo hadn't bucked she would have taken it away to Sweden, and it belongs to Britain," said Valerie, "not Sweden."

Fergie looked at Kristianne. "Is that true?"

There was a dreadful moment of silence while we all looked at the Swedish girl as she stood before us, her eyes averted from our gaze.

"Do you want to know the truth?" she asked at last.

"Of course," said Mrs. Gray. "We want to get to the bottom of this."

"It was put in my saddle bag to incriminate me."

"And who would want to do that?" asked the Professor.

"The man who knew that I knew he had taken it."

108

"And who is that?" asked the Professor craning forward like an elongated toad.

"The Russian, of course. Didn't you know, I had turned him down?"

"Igor?" I gasped.

"Who else?"

"And why do you suspect our good friend, Igor?" asked the Professor with the utmost seriousness. "Apart from the fact that you claim you have *turned him down*, whatever that may mean."

"Did anyone check his credentials? No, because Jake is little more than an ignorant peasant."

"Kriss . . ." began Fergie desperately.

"Carry on, please," said the Professor.

Kristianne cleared her throat. "Who is this man, Igor Polunsky? Why did he seek political asylum in your country? Why did he leave his homeland? Do you never ask yourselves these questions?"

"But this rhetoric doesn't prove he took the torc and slipped it into the saddle bag," the Professor objected. "And why didn't you tell us you knew he had stolen it?"

"Do you know that he carries Soviet propaganda?" asked Kristianne, with surprising composure.

"Oh, really, this is ridiculous," said the Professor, looking uneasily at Igor. "These accusations, these hints add up to nothing."

"You have never thought he might be a spy?" asked the Swedish girl.

"Of course not," said Helen Wetherall. "He is a very charming and cultured gentleman. If you have proof let us see it, otherwise please be quiet."

The Professor looked at Igor who had remained absolutely silent throughout, his face set, his chin sunk deep into his beard, his dark eyes brooding and his hands lying passively on Cadbury's neck. What was he thinking? I wished I knew: why doesn't he reply? I asked myself. His silence seemed to suggest guilt. Oh, Igor, please say something!

"All innuendo," said Eric Small, "to turn our thoughts away from you, Kristianne. I am sorry, but your remarks don't wash."

"And what proof do you have that he did not put it in my saddle bag?" asked the Swedish girl, with blazing eyes.

"It's your word against his, dear child," said the Professor. "Igor, what do you have to say?"

"Lies. A foolish and emotional girl has filled her head with rubbish. Now I will say nothing except in the presence of my lawyer—I understand your British laws, you see. I know my rights. What should I want with a torc? Do you imagine I want to adorn my neck? I am a man, Professor, not an effeminate boy."

"It is worth a mint of money, in case you have forgotten," said Jonathan, taking his revenge because sometimes he had worn a string of beads and thought Igor's remark about effeminate boys was directed at him. "And Russian refugees are not known for their wealth."

"Let's cool it," said Michael. "We are not going to get to the bottom of this. The main thing is that we have the torc back and can restore it to its righful owner. So come on, let's drop the subject and finish our trek in good humour."

"A real scout," said Jonathan mockingly.

"Here are your things, Kris," said Jane. "I'm afraid the eye shadow case is broken."

We rode on after Kristianne had remounted, our faces solemn and my feelings disordered and sad. I did not want to distrust the Russian, and yet the Swedish girl's remarks had made me wonder whether we should have

110

found out more about him. He could easily be an assaulter of women or a spy on holiday. And what about the Soviet propaganda?"

The Professor was wiser. "My dear girl," he murmured to me. "Our Home Office checks every person seeking political asylum with *enormous* care. I can assure you that he has been more fully investigated than anyone else on this ride. Kristianne is an ill-balanced child with more beauty than sense. This torc business is a terrible blow to her self-esteem. She has been caught red-handed and that is more than she can bear."

But all the same I wondered about the Russian's propaganda. No smoke without fire, I thought drearily. She must have seen *something*.

Felicity rode up to Igor.

"We are on your side," she said simply. "We believe you."

"Now my lips are shut. I have had enough to bear. First I am a maniac, then a spy and common thief." The Russian waved one arm in the air. "I am glad this ride is finished, for obviously in England a foreigner is not safe outside London. Fortunately I have a good English friend coming to pick me up and he will advise me on the action to take—slander or libel? It is a case for the courts. I will not have my reputation smudged, no smirched . . ."

"The girl's only sixteen," said Eric Small. "She's probably a nut-case. Don't you think you are over-reacting?"

"Thank you, no. My lips are shut."

Meanwhile, Kristianne rode ahead, looking like a young Grecian goddess, expertly controlling Caramelo, who danced with excitement at being so near home. They made an extraordinarily beautiful pair. And in contrast Igor looked like a great hairy bear astride a wooden horse carved by some peasant with a bluntish knife. Remembering how nice he had been to me, I wanted to touch his arm and say, "It's all right, every one of us understands that you are not that sort of person." Yet at the same time there was a sneaky little voice at the back of my mind saying, "What do we know of this man from behind the Iron Curtain?"

As we came down into Jake's yard we could see a long trestle table from the village hall laid for lunch, with tankards for beer and a bowl of roses in the centre.

"Very nice," said Mrs. Gray. "Very nice indeed."

And there was Jake with his leg in plaster and a wide grin on his weatherbeaten face, and his gaunt, aproned wife hovering by the house door.

Treasure neighed from a nearby field.

"Quiet, you old devil," called Jake.

We watered the ponies at the trough and started to unsaddle them.

"You've not cleaned the tack since I left then," said Jake with a wry smile.

"You took the saddle soap and rags," I said. "They went with your saddle bags."

"Not been washing the bits neither. I don't know, I reckon standards drop when I'm not around."

"He just wants to prove you couldn't really get along without him. Don't you take no notice, Sandy!" advised Jake's wife. "These men are all the same."

"Now turn the ponies straight out in the lower field. It's been shut up for four weeks so there's plenty of grass, and what they want most is a good roll and a bit of peace. Not surprising after living with you lot for the past six days," said Jake, hobbling in our direction. "We'll rest Fudge's hoof and she'll soon be well, I reckon. I'm glad to see you all back safe and sound. I hear the adventure included the arrest of our Russian friend here."

"Jake has no telephone, but he always knows what goes on within a radius of at least fifteen miles," I told Jane. "We think the woodpigeons keep him informed."

The trekking ponies rolled and stretched and rolled again, and then went off happily to graze, while Mimosa and Silverstar were put in the barn to lunch on oats.

"Now sit you down," said Jake, who seemed in a jovial mood.

A tall man with a bushy moustache and a small blonde woman with rosy cheeks now started to fill the tankards with beer.

"These are the fairies . . ." began Jake.

"Dad, if you call me that, I'll not stay here another minute, nor help you with them sheep tomorrow, neither," retorted the man, with a grin which seemed also to belong to Jake.

"That's my son, Jeff, talking straight to his dad, and this is his wife, Kathleen," said our friend. "And they've been taking the provisions to you, except on that one day when there was a bit of a mix-up, and Fergie's parents fed you all."

We shook hands with the man and the girl and made polite remarks about their food and fireplaces, before sitting down to a meal of roast beef, Yorkshire pudding, roast potatoes, new potatoes, roast onions and spring cabbage, followed by apple pie with cream or custard. And no meal could have tasted better. But all the time I was eating I felt as though I was sitting on a volcano.

Igor was eating as though each mouthful might be his last, his thick dark brows drawn together, his eyes moodily looking down at his plate. Kristianne, on the other hand, looked just the same as always and, although she ate little, she appeared to relish the meal.

"Well, I suppose you never came across that torc of

mine? Something of a mystery, isn't it?" said Jake, putting his elbows on the table and lighting a cigarette.

"I was wondering whether you would ask," replied the Professor at once. "We've good news, Jake."

"You've not found it after all?" Only Jake's quick uncharacteristic puff at his cigarette now suggested his intense interest.

"We have, indeed we have. Jane! . . ." The Professor waved one hand imperiously, and the elder twin stood up and waved the torc in the air.

"Jake, it's all yours."

"And where in God's name . . . ? Well, I'll be damned! I'd given up hope."

All our friend's composure had gone. He beamed on us, then leaped to his feet and literally skipped, plaster and all, round to Jane's side.

"It is and all, and I shall have that range of stabling after all, so long as the Government plays ball." He looked at me. "And we shall have a cosy little tack room that Sandy will keep tidy for me. And a holiday in Majorca for the wife. But where did you find it, Professor? I reckon someone deserves a reward." He held the torc in his hand, gently, as though he was nursing a newly-born chick. "You've polished it for me."

"The circumstances of its rediscovery are a secret and must remain so," replied the Professor gravely, before putting down his beer mug to wipe his mouth with a red handkerchief.

"All's well that ends well," added Mrs. Gray, pushing a bit of gristle to one side of her plate.

"My dear Mrs. Jake, I do congratulate you on your Yorkshire pudding," said Eric Small.

"I reckon it was the Professor, and he's too modest a man to confess," suggested Jake, looking quizzical. "Well, sir, thank you very much. I would have hated to lose it for good, having come across it with my own bare hands. That sort of thing happens only once in a lifetime, doesn't it?"

"Wrong," said the Professor. "It wasn't me. Now let's all be upstanding. I want to propose a toast. Let us drink to our good friend and leader, Sandy Hamilton."

There was a scrape of benches before voices murmured, "Sandy!" And then an awful thing happened, I burst into tears. It wasn't simply the thought that everyone was being so nice to me which made me howl, it was also remembering the quarrel between Kristianne and Igor. Worst of all was the suspicion that Igor might be a spy or traitor. Everything had been so fine until an hour ago and then . . .

"My dear Sandy, what is it, ducky?" Mrs. Wetherall was at my side, an arm round my shoulders.

"Overtired. It's been an emotional day. She needs a good night's sleep, that's all." Mrs. Gray took off her bowler at last.

"It's nothing. I'm a fool. Nothing at all," I said furiously, sniffing between my words.

"Let her cry," Igor said. "At times it's noble to cry and tears clean the wounds of the spirit."

"I was going to propose a toast to Fergie," said the Professor. "Will *he* burst into tears?"

"No," my brother said, "although I admit it's been rather a trying day, but I don't think I deserve one, that's all."

"I'll do it," said Michael surprisingly. "To Fergie, Master of the Horse."

Fergie blushed then and visibly stiffened as Kristianne touched his arm.

"And what about the map reader?" asked Felicity.

In the end we toasted everyone except Igor and the Swedish girl, whom no one could bring themselves to propose. Then Jake decided to put things right.

"We've forgotten our visitors from abroad," he said. "Come on, where's our sense of hospitality? I propose a toast to Mr. Polunsky and Kristianne, our beauty queen, whose looks and charm have inspired us all. Come on—cheers!"

He looked at Kristianne and winked. "Has anyone told you what a bit of sunshine you've been to us all?" he said.

"No," she screamed suddenly. "No, you cannot drink to me. I took the torc, and they are being so kind. They . . . they . . ." and then *she* burst into tears.

"Never!" said Jake. "Never, not our beauty queen!"

"I found it the same way as you found it, lying in the grass. I mean it belongs to whoever picks it up, do you not understand, that was my reasoning? I wanted to take a bit of old England back, and it fitted my neck exactly, as though it was made for me, as though it were mine. And then I couldn't, I just couldn't—so I accused Igor and then you drink a toast to us together. It is too much . . ." She paused, lifted up a tear-stained face, which was still beautiful, like a film star's when the owner is playing tragedy. "Can you forgive me?"

"Of course," Jake said unsteadily. "It was a temptation. We're all tempted sometimes and you were just not strong enough to resist just then, that's all. Now stop crying and spoiling our lunch. It's like what Mrs. Gray said, all's well that ends well." He lit another cigarette. "No wonder our Sandy was crying."

Just then the yard gate opened and a youngish man walked in with a smile on a wide, pleasant, sun-tanned face.

"Igor, my dear Igor," he called. "You look magnificent

116

in that get-up, and so *well*. You've missed your vocation, you should have been a country gentleman."

"Meredith! It's good to see you. You've found the place then."

The toast was now forgotten as we watched Igor jump to his feet and embrace the youngish man, who wore jeans and a shabby tweed coat.

"This is my publisher, a truly brilliant man," he said, turning to us. "And he's going to drive me back to London in his wonderful Lagonda—such a car it is. Meet Meredith Ramsay."

The man walked round the table, laughing and shaking hands with each of us in turn.

"A magnificent holiday," said Igor. "A little trouble to-day, but now it has gone away like a little black cloud and will not be remembered. I had a splendid horse, Cadbury. He goes in my next novel, even if he must become a Russian. He was like a nannie to me. I love that horse, Meredith. No, do not laugh, it is true. You will see him before we go. I shall take you across the field. Is your wife here? No, that is a pity, for I think she would love that horse too. He is the perfect gentleman. Now, about those Russian leaflets for the book—someone here thought they were Russian propaganda." He gave a great gusty laugh. "Well, I've brought a few to show you. I think they will go down well with the Russian emigrant community. And what about T.V.—am I to appear? . . ."

Watching the Russian and the young man talking I suddenly felt happy again. It *was* all right. He *would* forget it all and, as for Kristianne, well, only her pride had been hurt. She was too shallow, I decided, to be wounded for life.

"Just an overwrought teenager, think no more of it," Mrs. Gray whispered to me.

We had just finished all the apple pie and cream when Dad arrived with his mini-bus to take the train-goers to the station. He joined us for a cup of coffee and then Helen Wetherall shed a few tears as she bid Rolo a long farewell. "He's been such a darling," she said. "He knew his auntie was old and frail and treated her accordingly.

One by one, the trekkers signed the plaster on Jake's leg and shook him by the hand.

"Next year we come again, yes," said Igor, beaming like a friendly bear. "It has been a great experience, an eyesight into the British character, for me a triumph."

"There were times when I thought I wouldn't survive," admitted Valerie with a giggle. "All those creepie-crawlies in the straw and everything. But now I'm glad I came."

The Professor and his wife drove off first in their car, with Mrs. Gray at the wheel, still wearing her bowler hat, and Jonathan reclining on the back seat.

"I shall write, Sandy. It's been great," said Michael, wheeling his moped from the barn. "Much better than scout camp."

"You've been such a help," I said.

"Right, that's why I liked it. I enjoy being useful. You'll send me a Christmas card, won't you?"

"Of course."

He started his moped. "So long, then." He waved, looked back once then chugged away down the lane.

"Pop . . . pop . . . pop. I can't abide them machines," said Jake.

Kristianne took both Fergie's hands in hers, squeezing them gently as she gazed into his eyes. "Oh, Fergie!" But my brother's face was horribly wooden and his eyes empty of affection.

"Don't forget the Swedish holiday we planned . . . I shall

118

show you Stockholm. I shall be so proud of you my Scottish boy."

"Yes," answered Fergie solemnly, "I shall never forget." And I was sure that he was referring to the stealing of the torc. He turned his back. The girl stepped into the minibus. Dad started the engine. "Oh, Fergie, do wave," I said. "Don't be cruel."

He lifted his hand in a salute. "She never said goodbye to Caramelo. Everyone else took leave of his pony."

"Can we help wash up?" I asked, wanting to change the subject.

"Lord, no," said Jake's wife. "You've done quite enough." So then we went to the barn and tacked up our ponies. "Bags ride Silverstar," I said.

"I'm not worried who I ride," said Fergie. "Go ahead."

Jake hobbled over and thanked us, saying all sorts of nice things which I am not going to repeat.

Then we set off for home.

"I feel sort of flat," I said.

"Me too," said Fergie.

"Why didn't we find the torc when we searched the saddle bags?"

"I told her about the search before it happened. I never dreamt she might be guilty. She probably hid it in her sleeping bag. I told her *everything*."

"Never mind," I began.

"Yes, all's well that ends well," chanted Fergie in Mrs. Gray's voice.

"But it *was* an adventure, wasn't it? I mean the trek was worthwhile. I'm glad we went. Everyone was so nice, and so many funny things happened."

"Of course," said Fergie, "and I didn't really want to be special friends with her. I'm too young, I'm not ready, only she was always there."

We came to the bottom of the lane, where a stretch of grass runs by the side of the road. "Let's canter," I said. The ponies tossed their heads because they were nearly home. Mimosa gave a little squeak of pleasure and bucked and Silverstar bounded forward like a thoroughbred at the start of a race, but then came back on the bit like a properly trained dressage horse.

Reaching our lane, we brought the ponies back into a walk. Mrs. Grundell was sitting on her doorstep in the sun, her brown face as wrinkled as an apple which has been kept too long.

"Had a nice holiday, then?" she asked. "Been on the trail?" And we replied, yes, thank you, and told her the trek had been exciting and full of adventure. Leaving her, we came to our house, basking in sunshine, grey with white windows, standing between trees before a brown hill that rose like a camel's hump to meet the summer sky.

Learie was at the gate, his slanting eyes bright with welcome, and in the field Mimosa's yearling son let out a wild neigh of pleasure. Mummy came to the door.

"Oh, you're back, all safe and sound," she said.

And so we were.

If you have enjoyed this book, you will find lots more titles in Armada's Pony Parade to give you further hours of exciting reading.

Find out more about the wonderful range of pony books Armada has to offer, on the following pages.

DIANA PULLEIN-THOMPSON

A PONY TO SCHOOL
THREE PONIES AND SHANNAN

Two more exciting pony books by Diana Pullein-Thompson

THREE PONIES AND SHANNAN

Christina Carr has everything most girls dream of: rich parents, a beautiful home with a butler and cook, an Irish Wolfhound puppy called Shannan, and three prize-winning ponies. She should be completely happy. But she isn't. She's lonely, and longs to make friends with the noisy village children on their rough, unschooled ponies. They, however, despise her.

How Christina stops being a spoilt little rich girl, goes to riding club camp and makes a friend for life is an engrossing and thrilling pony story.

A PONY TO SCHOOL
The sequel to Three Ponies and Shannan

Christina and her friend Augusta are asked to school the skewbald pony, Clown. He is nervous and difficult, but they are determined to turn him into a happy, obedient mount. Then they discover why Clown's previous owners have failed to control him. The skewbald is a rearer – and if Christina and Augusta can't cure him of his dreadful habit, he will have to be destroyed . . .

Armada

Pony Care from A-Z

By Charlotte Popescu

Illustrated by Christine Bousfield

What is a hackamore? How much should you feed a
pony? How should you treat a girth gall? How can
you tell a horse's age?

The answers to these, and a thousand other questions,
can be found in this fact-filled encyclopedia, together
with all you need to know about grooming, feeding,
ailments, tack, grazing and stabling.

An invaluable, pocket-sized handbook – easy to look up
and with scores of clear illustrations. A mine of
information and helpful hints for all pony-lovers.

Armada

CHRISTINE PULLEIN-THOMPSON

PHANTOM HORSE
PHANTOM HORSE COMES HOME
PHANTOM HORSE GOES TO IRELAND

The three thrilling books by Christine Pullein-Thompson about Phantom, the beautiful, wild palomino whom no-one could capture.

PHANTOM HORSE

The story of how Angus and Jean Hamilton go to America, and catch their first glimpse of Phantom in the Blue Ridge Mountains. They are determined to catch him – but so are others, whose motives are sinister . . .

PHANTOM HORSE COMES HOME

Phantom is now Jean's greatest joy, but wildness is still in his blood – and when the family has to move back to England, Jean knows he'll never stand the plane journey. Halfway across the Atlantic, Phantom goes mad . . .

PHANTOM HORSE GOES TO IRELAND

A trip to Killarney with Phantom and Angus will be a wonderful holiday, Jean imagines. But it is not the peaceful place she expects. Strange noises are heard in their host's house at night – and then Angus is kidnapped . . .

Armada

JOSEPHINE PULLEIN-THOMPSON

SIX PONIES
PONY CLUB TEAM
ONE DAY EVENT
PONY CLUB CAMP

Meet the members of the West Barsetshire Pony Club and read about their riding adventures and hilarious escapades in four favourite books by Josephine Pullein-Thompson.

SIX PONIES

The Pony Club members face the exciting challenge of breaking in six New Forest ponies – and Noel earns a pony of her own.

PONY CLUB TEAM

The Major makes a bet that his team will win the Pony Club Hunter Trials, and runs a special training course for them. But with the Trials only a few days away, their riding is still hopeless ...

ONE DAY EVENT

A great day for the Pony Cub – and Noel is determined to prove that Sonnet is good enough to win ...

PONY CLUB CAMP

It's the high spot of the summer – as children and ponies arrive in glorious confusion at Folly Court to begin a week in camp. And there are some exciting surprises in store for them ...

Armada

'JINNY AT FINMORY' BOOKS

by Patricia Leitch

Armada Originals

FOR LOVE OF A HORSE

Red-haired Jinny Manders has always dreamt of owning a horse. When she rescues Shantih, a chestnut Arab mare, from a cruel circus, her wish seems about to come true. But Shantih escapes on to the moors above their home where Jinny despairs of ever getting near her again.

A DEVIL TO RIDE

Shantih, safe for the first time in her life, in the Manders' stable, is inseparable from her new mistress. But she is impossible to ride, and Jinny can't control her . . .

THE SUMMER RIDERS

Jinny is furious when Marlene, the brash city girl, comes to stay and insists on riding Shantih. But when Marlene's brother, Bill, gets into trouble with the local police, Jinny and Shantih are the only ones who can stop him being prosecuted.

NIGHT OF THE RED HORSE

When archaeologists come to Finmory to excavate an ancient site, Jinny and Shantih mysteriously and terrifyingly fall under the power of ancient Celtic 'Pony Folk'.

GALLOP TO THE HILLS

Jinny and Shantih become caught up in a desperate race to save Kelly from being shot for a crime he did not commit.

Armada

JACKIE

Pony Adventures

Have you read all these books by Judith M. Berrisford in Armada?

JACKIE WON A PONY
The wonderful story of how Jackie wins Misty – the pony she has always longed for.

TEN PONIES AND JACKIE
Jackie and her friends start up a riding stable. And despite some near-fatal disasters, the Christmas holidays end in a resounding success.

JACKIE'S PONY PATROL
When Jackie and Babs plan a holiday in the Pony Forest, they find themselves involved in a thrilling adventure – chasing a gang of thieves.

JACKIE AND THE PONY TREKKERS
Pony trekking in Wales for Jackie and Babs. But it's not the relaxing summer they expected . . .

JACKIE'S PONY CAMP SUMMER
Living under canvas, Jackie and Babs become involved in a bitter feud that nearly spells disaster for Misty.

JACKIE AND THE PONY BOYS
Why do the three show-jumping boys hate Jackie and her friends? The pony boy 'war' leads to accidents – and, worse still, a fearful quarrel between Jackie and Babs . . .

JACKIE'S SHOW JUMPING SURPRISE
Alone at Stableways, Jackie must ride to save the day – on a Grand National winner . . .!

JACKIE AND THE MISFIT PONY
If the lovely roan pony cannot be controlled she will have to be shot. Jackie is determined to save her . . .

JACKIE ON PONY ISLAND
What is the strange and frightening mystery of Pony Island where Jackie and Babs spend the summer holidays? The girls are determined to find out . . .